The Universe And
Earth

This is a work of fiction. Similarities to real people, places, or events are entirely coincidental.

THE UNIVERSE AND INSIDE OF THE EARTH

First edition. March 10, 2024.

ISBN: 979-8224404858

Written by Saymoon.

Also by Saymoon

The Universe And Inside Of The Earth

Table of Contents

Description

I am not a writer. just on this earth, I am exactly the same as you. but after the age of 13, I slowly started understanding this world as I grew older. Since then many questions arose in my mind. The search for answers to all the questions in my mind aroused excitement throughout my body. My curiosity to know about this world, space, Earth, Nature, humans and all the living beings of this universe had increased a lot. The way I am able to know this world, in the same way, whatever things came to my mind after seeing all kinds of happiness and sorrow in this world, I am telling only that to you all. I am writing all this only after seeing the behavior of this world.

I have translated this language, so if some words seem wrong then you all should understand.

Keyword

1. All the creatures inside this world
2. Nature- war
3. Great man
4. Humanity
5. Important
6. Money- rupees
7. Time
8. Believe
9. Freedom
10. Universe
11. Human
12. My own talk some
13. Women are the most powerful
14. The world is reality
15. The talks of own mind
16. Reality imagination
17. Tenses
18. All the problems of women
19. The reality of the book
20. Sexual freedom
21. Relationship
22. My mind
23. God
24. Stop the brain and mind
25. Compulsions
26. The reality of all human beings
27. Life

1. All the creatures inside this world

When I was 13 years old I didn't know much about the world. But many times I had definitely heard from everyone that he belongs to this religion, he belongs to the cast and country but no one ever said that just as we are human beings, in the same way he too is a human being who breathes, life is upon us. The same is on him too. But then after that when I turned 14, I was in 9th and 10th. What else is wrong about the hormonal changes and development of the student at that time in school? Is it true that he came to tell us all about the safety of these things? But there were some questions that if I asked someone, what would they think? At that time, I didn't even have a phone.

But still the questions that came to my mind had to be explored. While doing this, thoughts kept coming to my mind. Sometimes on religion, sometimes on earth and sometimes on the entire Universe, man is so helpless that what can he become in the face of difficulty and compulsion. Compulsion is such a thing that even if we don't want to do it, we get to do that work which we don't want to do. But one has to do that work under compulsion. No matter what the work may be?

2. Nature- War

In today's world, everyone talks about keeping nature clean, but we have been saying this since forever that the nature in which we live has to be kept clean. But why doesn't anyone think of this? Even when there is war, it is people like you who cause a lot of harm to nature. There are lots of bombs, guns, tanks, and nuclear bombs in it which is so dangerous. All that has been created by all of you, you should feel ashamed. You all say that you have to keep the earth clean and do it even after everyone knows. How dangerous is this bomb? Even after that, humans use these bombs, even though the sounds of the bombs are so loud. Due to which it has a deep impact on the hearing ability of a human being and not only does it cause a lot of damage to the ears, even the slightest mistake puts the entire body at risk from these dangerous bombs. Which destroys the entire life for a moment. Despite knowing all this, these dangerous bombs are still being manufactured, whereas the makers of those bombs are also in danger from them and at whatever place these bombs explode. There it leaves its effect for a long time. All the animals and creatures living there have to face many problems, but if we talk about firecrackers?

Firecrackers look very exciting and along with being exciting, they are also equally dangerous due to which many people have to suffer its consequences. This gunpowder is given in the hands of small children since childhood because most of the firecrackers contain only gunpowder, which causes a lot of pollution when the crackers are burst and along with the pollution, there are many accidents which lead to many deaths. Has been with. The sound of some firecrackers is so loud that it is dangerous for the ears of all of us and the pollution that occurs after bursting of firecrackers is very dangerous for all of us when we breathe and while bursting the firecrackers, how many people are also affected by it. Hands or faces get Burnt. Even because of such a dangerous thing which are small babies. Due to these sounds of firecrackers, the biggest impact is on those who make these firecrackers and many times many accidents happen to them too. He also gets injured. Because of these firecrackers, these dangerous firecrackers are still made by the person who is making these firecrackers. It is dangerous for all of them and for those who are using them, yet it is man who has created it and is also being used by man and it is man who has to suffer the consequences of all these. Then no matter who uses these firecrackers in the country, everyone will have to suffer because the country or the continent itself is different, but in which we all are living. He is the only one. That is our Earth in which we all are and we are the ones who are causing so much harm to this earth. Now all of you think whether these firecrackers are necessary for us or this earth in which we all are living and even if there are firecrackers then they should be such which do not cause much pollution nor loud noise which is safe for everyone, because these firecrackers everyone would love to burst. But if its consequences are seen then everyone has to suffer that too. This nature this earth has ever thought. How much she does charity for all of us. Never do favors. If we help someone even a little, we feel proud and feel that we have done a favor. It all comes inside us. But we do not think about the nature which is giving us the mother-in-law to live and so much to eat and drink. We are trying to destroy it unnecessarily. When bombs are used excessively, it spreads in the air due to which many people have difficulty in breathing and by using dangerous bombs, our soil also gets spoiled due to which even if some crops are sown, the crop gets spoiled. After getting spoiled, the crop reaches humans and after eating it, they get other diseases which cause so much harm to nature. Instead of making such dangerous bombs and spending unnecessary money on them, if you all spend money in saving the lives of helpless people or helping them, then only blessings will come for all of you and this will also make nature better, which will make human life happy. Will be. This nature which is so important for all of us humans that without it we all have no existence, yet we all humans are causing so much harm to this earth. This earth has always given to all of us only for our own selfishness. Never took anything. The day you all will feel this nature as your own and think deeply about this feeling. Then decide what is right and what is wrong because the day we start considering everything equal, only then we come to know that what we are is also the same. So now you all have to think. Is this nature necessary or these bombs and firecrackers which are so dangerous. Now it all depends on you.

3. Great man

Such great people also came into this world who have contributed only for the whole world. Not for any country, religion, race or any creature like Nikola Tesla, Isaac Newton, Einstein, all the scientists I like and many more. Nikola Tesla, who after working hard for many years, invented electricity, now he did not do it just for himself or for his country, religion, caste, removed the whole world from darkness and illuminated it which was not his fault. There is no selfishness, only he did it for you all, even if he is not there today. But whenever I look at the light of that bulb, my heart is always dedicated to such a great person and also to all those great people who saw every human being as a human being and helped all of them, not considering any country or religion and I would like all of you to consider everyone equally like these great people, and not on the basis of any religion or country or caste. How good would that be? If you don't like some of my words, then I Apologize to all of you, but whatever is coming in my mind, I am just writing it. Many things are awakening in me too, seeing the reality of this world, that's all. I am writing that in my mind also I feel like doing something for all of you which is for the good of all and no one gets harmed because charity is a very great word. I had read somewhere about a great man who did not do favors. Just doing charity I saw many ants catching an earthworm. Many ants were climbing and holding on to it and it was writhing in agony in front of me. Then I got that earthworm removed from all those ants and saved its life, which I felt was right. But then I thought how hard all those ants were trying to catch it and eat it. They are all hungry and this was wrong so I gave them sugar. As for food, this incident taught me that work should be such that no one is happy. Now you see, the only thing that comes from this is that if you are helping someone, then look at the other person who is working so hard and you can give him something so that he too becomes happy.

4. Humanity

This is most important "human" because everywhere in the world all the rules have been made by humans only and it is said that God has made them. In fact, I feel like crying so much that even today I am writing all this. Even then I feel like crying a lot. I didn't want to say it, but I am writing this due to compulsion from the whole world which is trying to destroy this earth. Taking advantage of false religion, they are engaged in destroying the entire Earth and my country, my people. Such people who do not think that all this will end here and one day we will all die. Earlier, when I was young, many people used to say that we were in danger from the country. There is danger from people of that religion. That caste is dirty, that person is not good and all of you who say this have these dirty thoughts ingrained in you. You see this also.

Earlier it was said that the people of one country will kill the people of another country. People of other religions will destroy people of other religions. But why doesn't anyone think, what is gained by bloodshed and how many poor people are killed? This earth is simply destroyed by war, slaughtered and poor people are killed in the name of religion and caste. Those who are innocent and then I also felt a little scared that at some places people of other religions live on the roads. Maybe he might let us beat him, but I was only 11 years old at that time. I was innocent. Didn't have much understanding of the world. As I grew up, I saw all the colors of this world, its ways, bitterness, jealousy, greed, ego etc.

When I was 13 years old, my mother, some of my mother's relatives and we all planned to go to the mountains. It was my first time. Well,my brother had planned to go but he didn't feel like going. Then instead of them, mom and I went, we also took some food items with us and we had to go there on foot. From the mountains, I climbed a mountain for the first time. First came a river bridge on the way, which looked very beautiful in the morning. The rays of the sun were falling on the river which made it look even better. There were ducks in it too. Then our journey started. We started climbing the mountain and there were many people who were going through the mountain. Then when we Reached the top of the mountain, we had come from there, the view was visible for a long distance, it was also looking very beautiful, then we moved ahead, at one place we came across very big stone rocks, from which some water was flowing in strong streams. After crossing this, I was very tired and also felt hungry. Then I had food on the way. After some rest we started our journey and then continued moving. Then there was God's place, then we went to God's place, then I was very tired due to going through the mountains and it was getting evening and it was raining lightly, our plan was to go home by vehicle. Then we bought some things there and roamed around that place. We went to the top most mountain. After going to that mountain, the clouds were touching all of us. This feeling was very good because it was the first time that I came to the mountain. And the clouds which I always dreamed of seeing and touching, were touching them in that mountain. I was standing there with both my arms spread, a smile on my face and the view from that mountain was far, far away. It was a great feeling. There again we went to the vehicle. There were only a few vehicles there and there was a lot of crowd. Then 5 of us decided to go by vehicle because we were tired. Some people who came with us went on foot through the same mountain path and we continued through the road. But we did not find any vehicle. We had come a long way and our home was very far away. It had also started raining heavily. We kept walking and then I started feeling a little scared. There were mountains and forests all around the road and night had started to fall slowly. We were just two Teenage boys, my mom and a mature girl and me. There were many unknown people on the way, then I asked God to help us, then we met two policemen on the way, we told them everything, then first of all the loaded vehicles were going on the way, then a vehicle came in which there were two men. One of whom was a mature person. There were others who were much older than them. The police told them to leave them and one of them was not well. My mother was also not well because of getting wet in the rain. Then we sat in their car and did what we were matured to do. He was driving and others were sitting on the other side of him. He started telling us that none of you is feeling well. My mother said yes, mine. Then he took us for a long distance through a hilly road. He stopped at a place, a hotel. He asked us to have something to eat and drink, we all refused, then they went inside the hotel, we all remained sitting in the car. Then we all got scared as to where we were left. Then after some time they came again when the mountain road ended and the City became visible. Then we all took a sigh of relief and the water bridge was shining very brightly at night, then after crossing that bridge, they had to go through another route, they dropped us, then we were giving them money, they refused, then we the humanity in this is that they could have done anything with us if they wanted to, but they was a very good persons, I don't know which religion they belonged to, which caste, but they came as an Angel of God for us. Who helped us so much that journey was a risk for me. Where will those people be now, but I always pray for them that wherever they are, they all remain well and all of you can also become such people who can help others without taking advantage of their helplessness and all of you the blessings of all of them will always be there. Like till today we all pray for them. I never see that this person belongs to another religion or caste, I just see a human being, just like I am, if you love them and treat them as equals. Then they too will love you, that is why it is said that humans have always loved everyone. We should live together, everyone should be considered equal, this is humanity.

5. Important

I want to ask all of you to tell me that you are at home in your country. If there is any problem at your home, is this problem happening because of another country and you people who unnecessarily use bombs and guns to kill people because the reality is that in today's era, the country which we live in is a state, a town and we say that this is my country. We will do anything for this. So there is no benefit. Because you all think this is my message to every human being. In this I am just telling you all. I am not blaming anyone in this. Just understand what I am trying to say. No, this religion, country or caste is not for him. Only for humans and this earth. Have you all ever thought that when there is rape, kidnapping and theft and murder, do people from other countries come and do the same? The people of the place where we are living do all this. Then why should we be afraid of people from other countries that they are a threat to us? Another important thing is that when someone stands on a post, the person standing on another post gets him murdered. As you all must be understanding, in today's times I have heard this word bullying from many people. At the age of 16, I came to know that I don't know how many people have committed suicide due to bullying and harassment. Now tell me, do people from other countries come to bully me and the most true thing is that today's world is rich. They do a very good job of making people jealous and humiliating those who are poor. Now my belief is that whether someone is a big businessman or a mechanic, for me every person is equal because that is why the work of both is different and both what a mechanic can do cannot be done by a businessman. Similarly, what a businessman can do cannot be done by a mechanic. Therefore, my request to all of you is that you should see the human being and not his profession because in this world God has created every human being in some way or the other. The best has been created for any work, so whether it is a small work or a big one, everyone should be treated equally and everyone works hard in the work. My hope from you all is that whether you people like this thing of mine, good or bad. I am just writing today whatever is in my mind which is real.

Once in my dream I felt that I was dying and my soul was leaving my body and then I realized that I was leaving without talking to my mother. Then I heard the sound of bells, a darkness. Then I remembered God and my eyes suddenly opened; indeed, parents are such an asset that no matter how much we say good or bad, they love us without any greed. My mother, when she got married, her family members listen, the neighbors as well as my husband, but my mother was harassed a lot but my mother did not give up, she fought that who would take care of my children after me and today I am who I am because of her, who survived all this. Is able to reach you. There will be very few people who can see the good of another human being otherwise there are many people who are so bastard who think of destroying another human being like these were the people who were very bad, my father was taught by bastard people who my father used to harass my mother as well as my in laws and neighbors. Now all of you tell me, when my mother was forced to die by so many family members and neighbors, did people from other countries come here? That's why I am telling you that even if you are from another country, will you trouble anyone? As many as there are houses on this earth, some people are helpless and troubled by their own family members and neighbors and not you people are doing it. The meaning of fear is shown to us by the people around us. And earlier it was said that it is not safe outside but to tell the truth, now no one is safe at home. If you can, then help all these helpless people by not looking at them with the eyes of fear but with the eyes of an Angel that there is one of our own who is there to save us all because it is very easy to kill. And saving life is very difficult, now all of you have to think about it.

Earlier, there were many greeds in my mind that I wanted this and that. But when I saw the accidents with my own eyes and saw people bleed-

ing, then I felt that there is nothing in this world, so why do we get greedy, we do not have faith for a moment because right in front of us, that happiness goes away in its vehicle. They were there and within a moment they were covered in blood, since then the greed in his mind had died down. Now it depends on you all that when will you die?
Today's world has made this accident its entertainment, which makes it difficult to believe anyone, you must have heard of many incidents. Somewhere there is a deserted road or where there are not many vehicles coming and going, many people find themselves when they get injured, they ask for help, then on the contrary, they kill the people who come to help them or do many things to them. In such a situation, the trust in others also goes away and those who actually ask for help from someone, then people hear about so many incidents. After this, we are not even able to help those hapless people and who does all this,man, God has created us all and we do so much to get something in this life, whether it is wrong or right, but we have to do it, it is our humanity. Forgetting this, he falls into brutality and for his crime, those other innocent people have to suffer the punishment who are distressed and helpless in reality. If there was humanity then it is within all of us but not everyone is able to help due to fear because of this. There have been so many incidents in the world that everyone from adults to children are aware of, hence due to this fear they and innocent people also have to suffer, who perhaps could have been helped because in today's time, trust is almost non-existent. No matter how much we trust anyone, we still have a fear that he might betray us or break our trust, which remains in the mind of every human being because of so many incidents. Want to do it but this fear remains in everyone's mind.

6. Money- Rupees

The word money and rupee are also for human needs. It is very important but have you ever thought that money remains but human beings die? Death is an unchangeable truth that we can buy many things with money but we cannot buy our death and life, so this shows that in this world. There is some extraordinary power which we can never see which is invisible but can also be felt and money is printed in different ways in all the countries and this is how the world runs and this money can never be used. We cannot eat, drink or sleep, but its importance is so much that you all know that existence is nothing but because of a rule it is identified that it is money, which is necessary for every human being. Depends on economic facilities.

Money, its importance is known to every human being on this entire Earth, but no matter how much money we have, there are many things which we cannot get back. The memories of all of us, whether good or bad, but the time. No matter how many times we remember the moments we have spent together and our mind says that I want to go to that moment just once, but we cannot go and the most important subject of life is called "trust". We trust someone. We do this after thinking a lot, but if he breaks our trust once, then he is no longer worthy of being trusted and the respect and honor that we have for him in our hearts Does not remain the same, even if he has everything and he give us money and try to make us believe but we are not able to do so and "Death" can we even say to god that you take the money and spare my life, it has become a bit of laughing matter isn't it because this is impossible in the God who he himself has given us so much, this body which is our soul, this body belongs to God and we are telling him only, and how beautiful are the memories of all of us, we remember every moment and then think that it is the same everywhere, so what if the years change and the body also starts changing. There are many countries on this earth where different currencies are hidden which are meant for

the economic convenience of that country, but it is said that we also have the currency. There should be, but we should not be proud of that posture because in life we should also have our own with whom we can share our happiness and sorrow.
He has a family, he has a lot of things, he has a daughter of 4-5 years and only her mother and father. They love their daughter very much but they say that there is not always happiness. Due to some compulsion, they have to separate their daughter from themselves. Now that innocent girl needed the love of her parents and the support of her parents. Today, despite everything, she still has nothing when she sees children being loved by their parents. She Misses them a lot, only tears remain in her eyes, only then she says that we need our loved ones more because they are everything to us, after all this. Even if we don't have that person with us, we become alone in this whole world and we say to god, what should I do with all this when I don't have my own people, so all of you respect your own people because every time is not the same, what is it every time? Only God knows what happens, that's why not only money is important in life, but people are also important, that's why we should love our own people too. As for money, it is always there, but how does a human being know when he will die? Money also remains but the human being ends. As the years are increasing now, I am also beginning to realize that where all that time is spent, every moment gone, today I have become so many years old, where are the remaining years. But things have passed, but this is the truth, now man will move forward, his memories of every past will come back sooner or later. When I remember those moments, I feel lost. But I see when I regain consciousness. You don't even have all that. Then I feel like doing a lot. Whenever I see that place to go to that moment, how it was there before and how it is becoming now. Then the importance of this money does not seem to be anything. In front of these memories because this is the reality. If you all are reading my story today, then perhaps you all might have gotten lost in your special moments while reading this book. I must have

felt for all of you too, but now when I look in front, you will be there, there will be something else but all that will not be there and after getting lost in the memories of our loved ones who have died, only tears remain in our eyes because everything is visible. Is giving. But that's not all, it feels like remembering every single moment of his. As if he would be with us. But when we look for them, they are nowhere to be found, so now you must have understood the importance of money. But today I am also writing one thing? I don't know the destination I am trying to achieve, but yes, I definitely know that I believe in God because this body which is not mine or the one who has given me this life, is my future. If I have seen the future then why should I worry? Whatever he does is for my good only with the help of him. There will be a time when you all will be with me, but just keep these blessings for me that I neither have any lust for the world nor any wrong feelings in my mind, I am writing all this as I am now, then also later. I should always remain the same, many questions come to my mind, my mind is that whatever I want to do for your all, I should just keep doing it, there should not be any hindrance, these are not dreams of mine, it is just my mind that I have to do it in reality because god knows every moment to come and in the future too, understanding every written word deeply and feeling it is the feeling in every word which you all have to understand.

7. Time

You all know this word very well. Because everything is stable at its place but where does the time go, whatever thing has come, one day everything ends. That time is over but memories are such a thing whose time is very powerful because from a child to a person when he grows old. When this happens, the age of his body increases but the memories of every moment always remain. He goes back to that time and thinks that I wish I could go back to that time and live that moment. Then I wish it could happen once again but the reality is that you also know that the time that has passed will never come back. You and I know this very well but if I wish it were so then I would really just want to have that moment of time every time. I went to the hospital to get an ultrasound done. And there were many people there, everyone was sitting, my mother and I too, my ultrasound was done, the report was yet to come, till then we remained sitting, I was feeling bored while sitting and started looking at everyone, everyone was tired of sitting and then I felt that there must be some activity or the other in a person's life so that he does not get bored in his life, that is why God has created all of us for every work, this also passes our time and we never get bored. We had gone for a walk. When I went there, a child was going with his guardian. He probably looked about 5 years old to me and some people were cleaning the place. Their children were also with them. Then that 5 year old child was happy to see the same cleaning children and was going towards them. Then the child was called by his guardian. Even then while going, he was seeing only those children. Then his parents came to him and started talking to him . Even while leaving, he was only looking at those children, that is why it is said that children are also like God, they consider everyone the same and do not understand any difference. But a child is also like water, just like if you put water in any object, it will take its shape, similarly, the child is raised and whatever is told to him, whether it is wrong or right, but he is brought up with the same ideas. Adapting itself just like seeing that child, I remembered that when I was 13 years old, it was my school's summer vacation, I went to my relative's place. He was in the army. At that time, he had got army quarters. I had gone there earlier also. But I knew the children living there, then this time when I went, I was looking at them first of all. The quarters of some of the families had gone to other places but some were my friends. At first I was feeling bored there because my relatives were there. There were only husband and wife and I. There were only three of us. Then after meeting some friends, every morning, immediately after breakfast, I used to go to play and then in the evening too, I used to play in the park, swing in the swings, have fun and cycle. There was a lot of fun in driving all of them, they all came from different states and our religion and caste were also different, but it did not matter to us children because for us, that child is the same as we are. There are other people too but some people, instead of telling their children that we are all human beings, what has happened if everyone's religion, caste, beliefs, lifestyle and speech are different, then instead of telling them that we are all human beings, that other person religion is dirty, caste is dirty, country is bad, etc.etc. by saying all this in the mind of that child, you teach all these things to the child and instead of seeing the other person as a human being, you tell them all these things. He will say the same things to someone else in the future, but children should also read this in school and should be told to everyone that no matter what country a person belongs to, just like breath and life are on us and our body is made up of the elements. He is also the same as God has created him, even if his country, religion, culture, way of life and speech are different, so what if he is a human being like us, then there will be no difference in the minds of every child and adult. In the eyes of everyone, every human being will be like them and there will be no fear. Then I came home after the holidays from my relatives' place were over. But after coming back from there, I was not feeling good at home, I was only missing my friends and relatives, I was not feeling good for several days, then I went to visit again, then their quarters had changed to another place. But I did not like it at all, then at night we went for a walk, then looking at that path, I remembered that the first quarter was here and I kept looking at the path only at that place, I was missing it a lot but I could not go. Because we had to go somewhere else, again when I was 15 years old, I went for a trip but I did not like it there at all and I came back to my home. No matter how many people we have, there is one friend, no matter what age. Why not, no matter the religion or caste, we are friends, even in such a crowd, we fall in love with someone, even if it is a stranger, but we fall in love and today I am writing all this, I am missing all of them. It is rightly said that no matter how old a person is, memories always remain fresh and at what time god makes him meet a person and when does that unknown person become his own, where would he be today and here I am a human being only a traveler. Wherever we go, we will meet many people on the path of life, but we hardly remember the faces of some people and one day life ends like this, all the time spent disappears with silence one day. Many people say that today is not our time. Today is yours, tomorrow it will also be yours, whatever you say, but what you say is always true, because in reality time is not always the same, because you can neither buy it, nor catch it, nor can you stop it. This is also an unchangeable truth, just like death is an unchangeable truth. I sometimes also think that when a person dies, how many struggles, happiness, or how he died in his life and how much he must have planned to do in his life but now his death. Actually, we think of doing a lot of things but sometimes we get disappointed, at that time we feel very sad and even cry and think why does this happen only to me, why does this happen to others. No, but believe me, in today's life, the rich person also has worries and the poor person also has worries. If you move forward thinking that everything will change in a few seconds and why should we worry, then how good it will be because of this matter of seconds. I am saying that I want all of you to be happy because no solution can be found by worrying unnecessarily, but by thinking, the solution can be found because no matter how much you all worry, but what is the use, one day all these worries will go away with death. Humans will die just saying all this that I have this and that, I don't have this and that and so on. Human needs everything which is absolutely true and to get this then what will he do? He himself does not know whether he is right or wrong, he just keeps doing that work, then he falls into such a problem, then he thinks why did he do it at that time, now I am stuck in such a time. Then he remembers his first time when I was fine, everything was fine, so I just had time and a few moments.

8. Believe

Trusting anyone has become a fear in today's world. That if we trust him, he might betray us. I think many times before trusting someone, if we trust someone, then if he breaks our trust, then we hesitate in trusting others too. We trust someone by considering him as our own, whether he is a stranger or our own, but when he betrays us, it hurts us deeply from within, the one whom we considered as our everything, loved him more than ourselves, We gave everything for him. Left and this is what broke our faith today. The words that come out of the mouth are also very amazing. You all know that we do not know what is going on inside someone, but the words from their mouth are good or bad. They start judging a person because if someone says something good then that person will listen to him and say that wow, what a thing he has said and if someone abuses him then he will say that he is such a dirty person, his thoughts and behavior in the world are different, everyone's attitude is different. What happens is that if something comes in this life, it lasts only for a few moments, days, months or years, then new things come, then people forget that thing and get lost in new things, this is the attitude of the world.

If a person dies then they make a wish for him for just a few days and then the world becomes the same as before and nowadays one does not even understand whether to trust one's own people or others. Because of all kinds of incidents. You all have heard and seen. Whatever I am writing. My only intention is to reach out to you that you should treat every person equally and not make any discrimination with him because. If he is also hurt, then bye the time the time of his death comes, you people will give him a daily life or by harassing and torturing him, then please let him live a peaceful life.

9. Freedom

There is freedom in every country. But still some women remain trapped in some rules and restrictions because in every restriction they are mostly told that one should not go to a deserted place alone, don't do this, don't do that, rest of you women are able to understand what I am saying. Whatever I am writing here will be about this topic because at some point or the other, all these accidents must have happened to all of you too. At some point or the other, we all have to go through these accidents. When I used to go to school, that road was deserted. It was my mother who always came to drop me and pick me up from school, but one day I had to come because the school was out early and I saw some men there and I got scared after seeing them. I was 14 years old and I came running very fast to the house and they were looking at me but that incident brought to my mind that why does this happen to us only, that's why we are women and taking this very thing into consideration, at ones and my neighbor's aunty we went somewhere to collect bushes for growing vegetables and while they were cutting the bushes, three or four men came there and started looking at us. I told aunty to go, but she did not realize that the man was they were looking at us only and our house was only 400 meters away from that place but it was a little deserted place, there were houses there too but not many, then after that my uncle and aunt came there, seeing whom the man got a little scared. And my uncle said, what are you doing here, go home because I had come to this place for the first time and had never gone alone, so that day I started crying so much that when all the family members started saying that even if there is only one man with the women, he is still a man, and even if there are two women with him, she is still a woman. Then I said, even if she knows martial arts, she said that one man is enough to spoil a woman's life, even if a girl knows martial arts, but with how many she will compete with, then I will have to face her. I got extremely angry with God. Why has God made us such that we cannot go anywhere without fear? I cried a lot that day and then I remembered that I should never go anywhere alone and I was very fond of nature. I like it more, even when we go for a walk, there is a fear that someone might do something to us. I think that if every human being considers himself a human being instead of looking at others on the basis of gender, then it would be so good. Hey, women also have a life, live it. Why do all of you force her to think so much? The more news is heard that a girl has been kidnapped, killed, raped, it is because of this that every women's parents and relatives are alert and do not even go out. Let go and the dreams of many women come to an end within the four walls of the house. Everyone thinks that only if women have security then they will send them out. However, in today's world, women have got a lot of freedom, but still, tell me, at some point or the other, all of you must have been afraid like I was, if all the man should also give the same respect to other women by seeing them in the eyes of their sisters, mothers and daughters, do not start teasing them by seeing them alone somewhere. Don't do this and think that yes, she is also the same, they also have the right to roam around, then there will be no fear for you man in the hearts of all the women, even some men who are very good, sometimes they have to suffer because of women. Problems also arise because women take advantage of the rules of law that have been made, due to which even good men become bad and because of this, these women put other women in trouble and innocent people are punished. It makes those who have not done anything also have to suffer all this and then there is a hindrance in making law and rules and then the matter continues like this. Then men say that we are facing problems because women misuse the laws made due to which those poor men get punished. Now you tell me which of the laws are made for the safety of women. Some women take wrong advantage of all these rules and get an innocent person punished due to which men lose their trust in all women. The same incident happens with all of us that some other man does it and we lose our trust in all the men and we. All women start looking at everyone from the same point of view. Now what you understand from this depends on all of you. I just said whatever was in my mind and I have said about both sides, not just one side and freedom. Which both want, not just one.

10. Universe

This is my most important subject. The universe in which there are so many mysterious things that just by thinking about them, I get lost in this entire universe. When it is night time and there is no noise, there is complete peace when I lie down and think about this universe that is apart from us. There must be other such planets on this earth which are inhabited by other living beings and they are at who knows how far away from us and as today we think of other planets while living on this earth, then perhaps the living being living on those planets are also something like this. When you think about the planets, when I think about the universe, there is so much inside this universe which only you all know today, then I think about whether this universe is also inside someone and similarly, what will be outside it. While thinking, I start feeling suffocated inside this earth. Everyday comes and every day I don't know how many questions arise in my mind and everyday and night all these questions bring enthusiasm in my mind because in my mind when questions arise, I become very restless in search of answers to them. The more I think about this universe, then it seems that everything is fine, but again and again I feel helpless because when I think about that universe, everything becomes fine. Okay, but all these other things and events happening in the earth, everything forces me to think about the struggling events inside the earth, even after trying every time to ignore the events of this earth and just focus on that. Even after thinking of trying to know more about the universe, it still forces me to think about this earth. That is why I have been able to write so much about humans today because as much as I used to ignore the events of this earth and the universe, I used to think then again and again that so much was happening in this Earth due to which I was forced to write all this, but now my mind is not so restless because I have faith in God. Now whatever he does, this universe gives me a lot to think about. But when will I know this whenever I am alone. And I think of the earth that there are so many human beings, everyone has a life and will we all really die one day, then I start wondering why do we die, where is the time that we as humans have spent so far, every single moment. It goes on, I get even more disturbed by this word death because every human being knows that one day or the other we all have to die but how we die, this word death is yet to be discovered. I want to know more about this, I get very confused about it, first I think of the earth, then the entire Universe outside the earth, then is the universe also inside someone? While doing this, who is inside whom, then I feel very suffocated. Sometimes I feel like this, when there is no noise at night and I try to sleep, then it seems that perhaps there may be more such creatures from some other planet which are at such a distance from our planet, but like you think about other planets, there must be such creatures in other planets too, who think, I don't understand a thing but today all human beings know that this is the Earth in which we all human beings are living, still why do we all fight unnecessarily. I feel like this, then even after knowing so much, what have you all been able to know, nothing? Still, this is a different country, religion, caste and I don't know how many unnecessary stories and fights you keep on killing and killing innocent people without any reason. Look, God has created all of us human beings on this earth, but our languages, appearance, way of life, culture of all of us, we all adapt to each other according to the place where we live, apart from this, the most important thing is that this is the nature without which our life is worthless. If it is not there then we will not even exist, which you all know, even after knowing all this, we humans are polluting this nature and trying to destroy it. But we are engaged in nature which is very good on its own and this universe. The more we think about it, the deeper we all get lost in it. Among all of you, there must be many people like me who have written all this. All of you must be thinking the same. If any of you are like this then I will be very happy. I will feel that it is not just me, there are others who think and feel so much and right now it is not just the universe but many things. Which

I have to analyze and know, there is a lot to do but everything happens with time when it's time comes. This time changes "is" to "was" with every nanosecond. That's how we are now. But if there is breath, if we are alive then we are human, if we are dead, then we are corpses. When I remember the earlier moments, it seems that everywhere we are the same, only our body is changing with time. What makes me laugh the most is that everyone knows that this earth is a planet on which all of us living beings are living. And apart from the Earth, there are other planets in the space and many things, but still man has to understand that this place on the earth is mine and it is yours, he has to fight to get that place, no matter what happens, so please do it and learn this thing. After all, what is the use of this planet Earth, we are living on it, how does someone else make something our right, there is no seal on it, but because of a right, it seems to be ours, in today's world there is so much technology. There has been an increase which you all know, still many people always misuse all these technologies instead of using them properly due to which other humans also face problems and that is because of doing so. I am very surprised to know about great human beings that despite facing every problem, they achieve their destination. Stephen Hawking. He also worked so hard that even after losing his body completely, he did not lose courage and we and many of you are such people that even if a small problem arises they create a ruckus, but there are many others who work courageously.

11. Human

In today's world, every person will either speak ill of another person or get jealous of him. Why don't we think while making fun of another person that how much he will feel bad that we are saying all this about him? At times, if a person is fat, thin, tall, short, black or has any other reason, people look at him as if he is not a human being but someone else. Hey, people like you should feel ashamed of making fun of others and also always remember that at one time someone is strong and at the same time one can also be weak because sometimes some incidents happen when we regret what mistake we did which resulted in this result because God gives every opportunity to the human being. But when he doesn't, God doesn't even give him a chance to repent. Sometimes, due to some accidents happening to humans, some changes occur in their body. Instead of helping them, people make fun of them, but there are also good people who help that person after seeing his condition and do not make fun of him. That's all I want to say to all of you, those people who are already sad after seeing their body, then you all should help them. Do not make people sad or forced to take any step which is wrong for them because God has created us and all of you for some work or the other. Now you all can think for yourself that if all the human beings in this world become the same, then what will be left to identify and differentiate between human beings? I hope that you all will be able to understand what I am writing. And if you like it, if all of you show your love just like the words spoken by me, then I will truly feel that I and all of you have succeeded in whatever efforts I have made for all of you, that's all for me. It will be a priceless gift. I myself am very afraid of making fun of someone because today I am making fun of him and if tomorrow even worse happens to me, then behave well with everyone because death is going to come for everyone today. Otherwise, everyone has to die tomorrow, my mind gets disturbed, then I think that in a moment we will all die, then what we are living now is just for some time, so if we do not help anyone, if you can, you should not bother that person. Today I have this hand, whether it is thick or thin or whatever, but because of its presence, I have been able to write so much. If it was not there, then whom would I tell, who would help me to write so much? Now think for yourself. You are reading the words written by me, you mean my book and not my hands, therefore look at the work of a person, not the structure of his body and such people should be encouraged more, who have any problem in their body, they should not be discouraged because god is everything. Let's see some and now I would like to say to those people to whom God has given all the body parts but because of their complexion or being fat or thin, they remain sad with their body everyday. God has given a body to all of you and the hormones of our body do not always remain the same. As we grow older, our body also keeps changing and changes keep taking place in our body. With the passage of time. This is the body. What accident can happen when? Who knows when the body will become fat? Thin but it depends on what people see at present, so what is there to be disappointed about. Be happy with yourself, spend every moment happily and if your body wants to grow from child to young and from young to old, then instead of being sad about your body, be happy. Live, at least God has given all the body parts and senses to all of you. Just ask those who do not have all these, the humans who understand the importance of all these body parts, but in the future, what deficiency will come in our body itself? You may not even know that you may have seen many such people in a couple in which one of the members of the family is damaged but the other person does not care about it, they live their life happily because it is important to have love in life and a person's behavior because in life there can be problems in a person's body but his behavior is not in love due to which the other person understands him and both of them live together and spend their life happily because in life only if we are human. If you love after seeing beauty, then it is love only as long as the body is beautiful. But if we love a person after seeing his behavioral qualities, then that love will, remain forever, even if some part of that person's body is already damaged or his body gets damaged later, but that love will remain forever because the person has only his body has changed, not his behavior, he is the same as he was before. There is a couple, they like him because of his behavior and with time, if something goes wrong with his body, then will you all leave him, then never because this is happiness and sorrow. So it is with everyone and it can happen with us tomorrow too. Even if you want to leave, do not leave by taunting the person about his helplessness because that person will break because I understand that every person has his own compulsions in such situations, that is why I have written this topic. I thought it necessary to write this also so that those who harass such helpless people can understand very well that today there is nothing wrong with your bodies, so you all make fun of those helpless people,God somewhere in your bodies, those poor people, don't do anything more than people, so never harass anyone. If you can't help, don't harass them. And all of you, to whom God has given all the organs and senses of the body, also be happy because all the time. Your body will not remain the same as it is now, it will keep changing with time and you all should be happy that God has given such an important body to all of you, through which you can do any work without anyone's help. Ours is the most precious thing in the world. Everyone has the same body.

12. My own talk some

Today I am telling some of my sorrows. I was undergoing treatment for my first stone which was completed then the doctor asked for an ultrasound but along with my stones an ovarian cyst was found which the doctor said might require an operation as well. It is possible that treatment can also be done. I was a little scared after hearing about the operation, but the doctor advised me to go to the gynecologist, only he will tell you whether there will be an operation or treatment. Then I explained to myself that everything will change in a few seconds. That's why one should never worry and whatever has to happen will happen. Then I felt a lot of pain during the night. My mother also took care of me but I was thinking that when the morning comes I will go to the gynecologist. Only when I go closer do I say that the pain is such that if unable to bear it, feel like dying, then this person who is fond of the color of the world does not like anything. If the external wounds of every person are not visible, then it does not mean that he is do not suffer from inside the body, then the next day we went to the gynecologist, told her everything and she gave me medicine for 5 days and then also asked for ultrasound, then I was taking the medicine but was in pain because my cyst was painful.

Then after completion of 5 days, I got the ultrasound done in which my cyst was completely cured, only the stone was still there, that is why it is said that one should not make the mind sad and let's see what happens next because whatever happens to me in the future. God knows that it will happen, otherwise I don't know. Then why should I worry? I am also writing this book after seeing all the actions of the world and their circumstances because I see how much of this book I will be able to write, but whatever is in my mind. I am just writing all the same things. Now after hearing the doctor talking about the operation, I got a little scared and remembered why I was scared. Whatever has to happen will happen, so I don't worry and everything changes in a few seconds. Which you all know and you should never feel sad or give up in life. Keep trying as much as you can and do the thing in which you feel like, no matter how much anyone forbids you, but that work should be such that no one else can do it. Don't be worried at all because you got the benefit of such a work in which you are happy and many people are worried because of you, so you all should be happy and don't worry.

When I was 15 years old, there were 15-20 minutes left for the school to be dismissed. At that time a very strong storm came and heavy rains and winds started blowing, due to which the school was dismissed and everyone started going to their homes. One of my classmates asked me to go on the vehicle. We started going on the vehicle. There were fallen trees on the road due to the storm, then we came from another route, there were also fallen trees there, then we came from the third route some distance. I was home, then on the way, school children told me that your mother is going towards school, then I started going towards school again, I met an uncle on the way and for the first time I sat in a vehicle with an unknown person, then he was nothing. He said, when we took him further to the road, I saw that the same trees had fallen, so I got down from the bike, then I thanked him and went ahead, then I reached school and saw that mom was outside the door, then I went to her, bye then the rain and storm had stopped. And the sun came out and I was very angry at mom. Why did you come here because mom used to come to take me half way there, where there was a deserted road and that day she had reached school and I was feeling very angry. I was scolding mom that I had to go back to school because of you. Mom said that it was raining so much, I had brought an umbrella for you so that you would not get wet in the rain, but ignoring her words, I was just I was angry at them all the way that what was the us of an umbrella, it was so sunny and I was angry with them and then we came home. But later I realized that I was wrong, my mother came so far to school just for me so that I do not get wet in the rain and my health does not deteriorate and how did she know that today I was going in a vehicle with someone else and the next day one day, when I went to school, all the children who saw my mother going to school were saying to her that your mother has come so far just for you, your mother is very good who loves you so much, so I also have to admit my mistake. But there was a lot of realization and regret and I felt that it was right that only those who are lucky, God gives such a loving mother who takes care of me a lot, loves me a lot and understands me, so all of you also never hurt those who love you so much because it is very difficult. You meet someone who loves you so true, otherwise you will meet someone who will destroy everything in the world, or he will be with you with all the meaning, and if the meaning ends, then togetherness will end, but the one who loves you without any meaning that this is the true love, he will care for you because if you all of you get angry at them, scold them, still they will care for all of you and take care of you but the world will love only out of greed and not unnecessarily, so all of you understand those people and that relationship can be with anyone which is just for you. Instead of taking only these prayers from God for all of you, God will always keep them fine and if you tell them that you want something from me, then instead of wanting anything they will only want you and say that if you are fine then I am also fine and everything is received. So this is true love and what kind of love is that which keeps on taking something or the other from you every time just to fulfill its needs, even if you are in any problem, despite not seeing your problem, it insists on fulfilling its needs only and gets angry. When you can't fulfill their needs, then whom would you like to respect, the one who cares about you unnecessarily or the one who is with you only to fulfill his needs?

13. Women are the most powerful

In this whole world, women have to struggle with every challenge, but there is one more thing which happens to us even if we are not worried about it, even then we still get worried about it, the menstrual cycle which every woman faces when she reaches adolescence. These happen. And end only in old age, but we have to endure this menstrual cycle every month and its pain makes many women helpless. I was one of them when I was 12 years old. At that time, I did not understand what is was and what it was not, but my family members only told me not to eat food that heats up a lot, non-veg eggs, otherwise you will get heat, I understood that heat meant prickly heat and that all these prickly heats were caused by heat stroke. You might be saying that because I use to eat to boiled egg cutlets everyday and also used to eat a lot of non-veg, due to which everyone in the house used to say that I would just get hot because the weather was very hot, then in the beginning I did not know when it happened. Then I asked my mother, she said that this is the menstrual cycle, I was a little scared that it happened to me at such a young age, then my mother started saying that you used to eat hot food, so then I said, then why didn't you tell me clearly? If all this happens then I urge all the family members and anyone else to openly tell the children about this so that they can handle it because hence they will not get troubled in any way. When I initially had menstrual cycles, they would last for 10-11 days. And that too was very much and if she was 12-13 years old then it is childish where she doesn't have so much understanding and then she also has to go to school and my mother used to wash the clothes which got stained due to period and my mother used to wash my clothes very much. It used to help. There was a lot of pain and bleeding during periods. At that time, I used to think that we have to endure this problem every month and during periods, I could not sleep even at night and my clothes would get stained. I used to go and for 2 years, my periods were only for 10-11 days because I still ate non-veg egg cutlets. Maybe due to getting too hot, you get more periods. Then now I started getting only 5-6 days. Then I heard from many women that some have less days, some do not have pain, some told one thing and some others and everyone told about themselves that harmons of all women are different, which you all know and whatever I have to bear. Many of these women must be like me who must have endured all this.

Once upon a time, I always celebrated the festival of God at night. I started going there at the age of 12. I used to go there at night. I celebrated this festival from the age of 12 to 18. I did not have periods at that time and I like this festival very much. This time when I turned 19, this festival was about to come, which is my most favorite festival among the festivals of the whole year, so I was having periods. It had been 6-7 days and I was about to get clean, so I was happy that today I have to go to my God, but when I went to the washroom, I saw that I was not completely clean yet, so I started crying a lot that this what kind of a rule is there that the people of the world call the thing which God himself his given to women as dirty, that in such a situation one should not go to God. I cried a lot at that time and kept asking God why such a thing was created. Because of which I could not even meet you but the festival was at night so by then I had become clear but that day a question came in my mind that the thing that makes up the world has many rules in it and I said this. It is also known that the rules regarding the time of periods are different for different religions and castes, due to which many women are also suffering from these rules. Women of different countries, religions and castes have been suffering from periods for a long time. They also do work along with them, whether it is at home or outside, but they do it along with them and they also do it with this problem due to which they all remain troubled. There are many countries where women who go out to work are given 2-3 days leave, at such a time all of you think how good it would be if this happened all over the world. Now I am saying that this thing of mine may seem strange to many people and very good to many people and perhaps many people may also raise questions on this, so please I want whoever is reading this to I am just writing what is on my mind, so no one should bother me, they will be intelligent enough to understand whatever I am saying. If there is such an injection which can start and stop the period, then how many of you will be happy because the main function of period is to remove dirty blood from our body, which is clean blood and if there is excessive bleeding, women become very weak. And the most important reason for periods is that everyone in the world knows that the menstrual cycle is the process by which a child is formed from an egg, which is why it is very important, so the thought came to my mind that it is important for the child. If it happens for a reason, then why should we bear this pain unnecessarily every month, because today's generation has progressed so much, so we can do the same when a woman is about to enter adolescence, after 11 years, at that time a the injection should be given in such a way that the menstrual cycle stops the eggs in the same ovary cover and when we need a child, then another injection is given so that the period occurs and after having the child, if the injection is given again to stop the menstrual cycle, then all the women women will get freedom from the menstrual cycle, then they will be able to live everywhere without any worries and will be able to go anywhere because wherever one goes, when the date of menstrual cycle is about to come, everyone is just worried about when will it happen. Otherwise, after getting this injection, I am feeling so happy just thinking about it without any worries. If this happens, then you all know that it is going to happen, so I have a lot on my mind for all of you, for the whole world.

14. The world is reality

Every person in this world needs arrangement for everything. Everything which is pleasant for his life, a person always wants to get more happiness and less sorrow, but perhaps we never know what is going to happen in our destiny, so we think that there are many things, but.... In my mother's back. She was having pain since 3:00 in the morning, even after applying balm, mom's pain was not getting cured and mom was also feeling like vomiting, then in the morning we took her to the doctor, then there after giving injection and medicine, my mother got better but around 6-7 o'clock in the night, we were eating Apple, then we also gave it to mother, during this time she felt very cold and her body was shivering, then we massaged with oil and mother. I was taken to another doctor and then given injections and medicines and my mother also vomited a little. Then again in the morning when my father had gone to work, then at around 10:00 my mother felt the same shivering all over her body and started telling me that she I called my father and told him, then I told the doctor in the call, then he said to feed the medicine to my mother, then after feeding the medicine, I started massaging my mother's feet with oil, but my mother started telling me that either God or kill me or do it right and she started telling me to take care of myself, then I told her not to say that, everything will be fine, then mom was saying some emotional things and was agonizing in front of me due to which I again started crying a lot and hearing my crying, my neighbors came, by then my father had also come from work, then we took him to the doctor, he got an injection, then the doctor said that if the severing happened again, there would be a blood test, but that day, mom seeing me in such a condition, the beauty of the world was not looking good at all and I told my God that if something happens to my mother today, then I will never talk to you after today, really nothing in this world will happen in a moment. There was a lot of happiness and a lot of sorrow, then that day my mother got a little better. And my grandmother had also come and I shivered again during the night. Mom started saying the same things due to which I remembered God. I knew that everything changes in a second, but seeing such a situation in front of me, I felt very sad. Well, mostly I was crying because my mother was saying emotional things to me, then I had put the status of my mother on WhatsApp asking everyone to pray for my mother to get well because God sees the blessings also. Therefore, due to the prayers of all of them, my mother got a little better. Well, what can I say thank you to all of them, they all are my own. From 11:00 in the night, we went to sleep at 2:00. When mom got a little better, then mom's blood test was done in which there was only deficiency of iron, vitamin, hydroxy, then the doctor gave me medicine based on that, now my mother is fine, I had full faith in my God, what could happen, but perhaps this test was taken on me also so that other could only then will we be able to understand the pain and this doctor is also very good whom I consider to be good person because he is a very good and noble person whom looking at me he seems like one of my own to whom I tell everything without any hesitation and he they never get angry, never scold and respond to everything by listening carefully and understanding it, and hence I pray to God to keep them safe and well because only if they remain well, we too will remain well because to take care of us. God exists and this too.

15. The talks of own mind

Till now I have not been able to find any person who can be my best friend, who can understand me and also I can tell him whatever thoughts come to my mind and then he can know the things in my mind, what I want and what not. And till now I have not been able to find anyone whom I can call my own with full rights because how does a human being know that in one moment he can become his own and in the next moment he can become someone else's, so this is my life, my body is only God's and not mine. It is he who has created me and after doing all the purpose for which I have been created, there is no fear even if I die, but whatever I want to do should be fulfilled for all of you, after that my real home is God. I will go to them happily and peacefully. Sometimes I get very confused. Firstly, I believe that this earth is a planet, outside there is the universe which makes me think about the scientific world and when inside the earth, when I see some incidents then everyone says it is only for God that we are there, then there must be something extraordinary and now I feel scared even if I trust humans too much, how they feel like me in a moment due to their words. And then the same person disappears in a moment, then I cry a lot remembering that person, I remember spending every moment with him, who used to do a lot for our happiness and to whom we gave our time. I considered him my own with full rights, today after sometime he became a stranger there and life is this time, today I am here, tomorrow is where, I talk to everyone with love just thinking that who may have seen me yesterday or not, but in the future. How is it that old friends get separated, then new friends are found on the road, but those separated friends are always remembered, just like the leaves of a tree, as old leaves fall, new leaves grow in them. Then we should learn from this that perhaps the person who was with us was with us till the time we had, now it is someone else's time with us and we should accept this and never be disappointed. And this is the world, we don't know when and what accidents will happen. When I know, I think that everyone is going to die and whatever is going to happen in the next few moments, then only god knows it, I think about the paranormal. When someone says that something is abnormal then I struggle with every single incident inside the earth and when I just think about the universe and every planet and what happens outside the universe then I struggle with it. Then I get very surprised and then I get entangled in this dilemma. Then my mind tells me that I should trust only these two because perhaps that is why I feel this way after seeing all this in front of me, but sometimes I feel like this. It seems that whatever activity happens on earth and whatever I feel or know in front of me, whatever I understand from it, it seems to me that God has created me in this world so that I can explore the world. And perhaps the day my book will be published, I will feel that my goals have started being fulfilled and I am slowly reaching that destination and there is still time, perhaps because I do not have that understanding right now and the world has to be explored and I do. That's why I am coming, whatever you have read, I have been able to write all that only when someone has some problem in his body since birth, still I feel very sad to see this, I think that I should do as much as I can, but his sorrow will always be with him but there is also a question in his mind that maybe I should do something else. But my mind feels so satisfied that at least I have done this much, I was able to give them peace and happiness, but I feel more regretful about the fact that the body we have right now is fine and which part of it might get damaged. Whenever I see someone's amputated hand or leg or any other problem in that body, then I think that this is also a human being, who despite being helpless with his body, faces every difficult and difficult time. God has given a human being. Everything in this world has been given to us which is very precious, all the organs of our body and senses, still we keep telling God that what has God given us, how is the game of time, I don't know why the mind feels restless. Whatever I am writing, I start to feel strange in it and then I start writing, till the time I keep writing whatever comes to my mind, just like I am writing now, now it is like this, I am also beginning to feel that whatever happiness or sorrow I have seen on this earth or the behavior of human beings in this world, I am hardly able to write this much till now, when I write whatever comes to my mind. Then the mind becomes calm. I have seen many videos and heard from everyone about aliens and time travel. In the videos, it is told about many people that have come after time traveling and they are aware of the upcoming events. They also predict that all this will happen on this date, month, year, I don't know whether it is true or false, but I know this much that I believe that humans are already aware of what is going to happen in their life. By narrating the incident, it is to create unnecessary trouble because it creates chaos among the people and there is a fear that all this will happen and then the person starts worrying unnecessarily every moment and due to that, every moment he gets stressed, he does not have anything to live for. I have met him and one day he dies just because of this worry, but I believe in God. Because we have seen our past, seen our present, but not the future, and whatever is going to happen in the future, we worry about it. We create a lot of fear in our mind, but what is going to happen is not exactly what we think and reality is. There is a huge difference in time travel, so now what you all think, it depends on you all. I have only told you what I believe and there is a lot more in my mind about time travel which I want to tell you all. But before that I would like to know how much love this book gets from all of you and most importantly about the aliens. I will tell you about it in my second book only, for which you will have to wait. However, I believe that the Earth is a planet in which I and you all are like this, the universe is so big that we can't even imagine, similarly there must be other creatures living on other planets too, but I will write about more things in this subject in my second book only.

16. Reality Imagination

Have you ever thought that it is just an Earth? But in this there are many continents, then countries, then states, then districts, then cities, towns and I don't know how many towns, and on this one Earth we are all human beings, but we all have many more languages and dialects which you all know as many languages as we do. Everyone must know only the same thing, we will be able to understand what someone else is saying, but if someone else speaks a different language then we will not be able to understand it, so think for yourself, when a person does not know how to speak a language, then many people make fun of that person. Sometimes think to yourself how much language do people like you know that you insult another human being? People like you should be ashamed because all you people do is make fun of others. Also keep in mind that there are many languages in this world, so do you know them all? Then it is also expected from all of you that if a person does not know any language, then you all should help him and not make fun of him. Humiliate them, there are so many countries on this earth and so many types of people live their lives in that country, but what is most important to understand a human being in this life is their language. Until no one calls it a language, we will not be able to understand, but I don't know, due to being humans beings inside this Earth, they all have different dialects and languages, which becomes quite difficult to explain that how will we be able to learn so many languages, everyone's alphabets, words, letters are different. Every single thing of a human being starts from this and it is not necessary which country's religion the child belongs to but it is important where he is being brought up because the human mind is like a machine. Just like a computer can store whatever we want in it, similarly we all have a brain, whatever we learn and know, our brain starts storing it, due to which all the types of humans we are, we have our languages, when we are small children, he understands our language and starts storing it and small children have a large number of neurons, at that time whatever is taught or told to him, he starts storing it in his mind very quickly and then whatever he receives. If we tell, then it is not important in which country, religion or caste the child was born, but where he is being nurtured, it is important, but not only human beings but also the other creatures, animals there belong to all of us. They understand languages because they are nurtured with all of us, due to which their brain also understands the language of us humans and stores it in their brain, hence language is important only for humans, animals, creatures. Like there are many medicines which a man uses whether he is married or not, but the effect of those medicines will be on the body of both of them because the effect of the necessary medicines has to be on the body and not because of the man being married or not. The place we are living in is important in the life of all of us because all human beings are equal to God. Because whatever we say to them in any language, they also understand what we say, that is why God has created all of us, but there are so many experiences and feelings in this body which we all can feel. There is energy in our body too. There is a feeling which makes us feel about any action or any moment that something wrong is going to happen to us. Most of the feelings which occur are a different kind of feeling except the happy moment, which all of you have also experienced in your life. We must have felt this feeling many times in life, like when we meet many people unknowingly, then when the behavior of some unknown person seems different or their behavior is strange, we become uncomfortable, our body feels in a strange way. This shows that there is a lot of power in the senses of our body which evaporates anything and gives us a signal that this unknown person is not right, but why should it be an unknown person, even if someone is our own. We all understand that because of his behavior and our mind brings so many unnecessary thoughts, all of which are imaginary and are unnecessary, as soon as we all wake up from sleep, from that very moment, who knows how many, thoughts keep coming to our mind in this mind due to which sometimes we get disappointed or even start having headache because all of them are imaginary, however, we should pay more attention to the real because what is real is the truth. Therefore, we should see the real world and our attention is the most important thing. The biggest key in life is the "attention" of all of us human beings because if you spend your time thinking about imaginary things all the time. If you waste it then you will always remain in the world of imagination but if you focus your attention on reality then you will be able to understand everything because this body is yours and you have to control it. And thoughts come while awake and dreams even while sleeping. This shows that our mind keeps bringing these thoughts all the time and some imaginary thoughts are good because only when thoughts come, questions are formed and answers are searched only on questions. But if imaginary thoughts are for your good then it is fine but if some imaginary thoughts dominate you then it is wrong, therefore if you get unnecessary imaginary thoughts then try to keep yourself busy with someone else. Do some work or think at work so that your attention goes somewhere else and do this several times whenever unnecessary imaginary thoughts come, in such a situation you will learn to control yourself and more imaginary thoughts will not come and time will not be wasted. It will happen and you all will also be happy, one important thing of the body which is most important is faith, which means not believing in anything even after it happens and keep encouraging yourself, every strength of man is based on our faith. It happens that if you don't have faith then you won't be able to understand everything, like you have to achieve something and don't know how many people refuse that what they want to achieve, they will not be able to get it, but the body of all of us, even if many people refuse, our body itself should not tell us that it will not be found and we should have faith in God that it will be found no matter how much time it takes. But you will definitely get it, that is why it is said that there are many obstacles and there are so many restrictions, but before the words of others, you should have faith in yourself. If you have faith in yourself, you get everything but not by forcing someone because it is in our body. There is a positive energy which is based on belief because our body is with us which has made us believe, we start getting an experience that whatever we are waiting for, we will definitely get it one day. It is like the belief of getting one's wish or getting someone that one day you will definitely get it, no matter how many people refuse to let it be, your body still assures you, you feel that you will definitely get it, you hear from someone close to you that he is a criminal or he died somewhere but even after that you are sure that he is alive and not a criminal and you start searching for him and finding out about him and people all deny it. But if you don't know why you believe that he will be alive, then this belief is a positive energy because even when everyone refuses, we believe that it is not the one who is saying all this but believe in yourself, well that's how I am. It has been together and has also been completed, which I will tell the whole story of this belief in my other books, that is why "Believe in yourself because belief is everything".

Many people are like this, if a person does a little something wrong, then they start criticizing and insulting that person as if he knows everything in the world, then you also think that the person who you are humiliating that person in front of everyone, how bad that person must be feeling and God has definitely created every human being for some work, so maybe he could not do that work, made a mistake, but it is not necessary that he and if you are not the best in your work, then those who insult others should remember that it does not take long to change the time and now you have insulted him, tomorrow someone else can insult you even more, I will not refuse to explain. I am explaining it because if someone commits a mistake it is very important to explain it so that he cannot commit any mistake in future, but humiliating a person in front of everyone hurts and hurts that person a lot. Now you all feel the same way. Do it because every person is not the same because a person also sees and tells about the actions and behavior of the person who has committed a mistake, which is for his good so that we cannot commit any mistake in the future like our parents, relatives scold us after committing any mistake and explain it to us so that we can understand so as not to commit any other mistake. But sometimes we find his words wrong and we insist on our own will, but still he makes us understand because he is his own who cares that we do not fall into any trouble, that is why he is yours without any greed or without any meaning. If you love, explain, then you must obey him and he can be anyone from your parents, relatives or friends. Now God cannot come to us, but he makes himself available in some form or the other when we are in trouble or sorrow. Or when we are happy, then in some form or the other, he is definitely with us in these forms.

17. Tenses

In this world, our whole world runs in these three times - past, present and future, which you all know, the past which has passed cannot be brought back, the present which is now and the future which is the time to come. Who has seen when in a nanosecond the opposite of what we thought happens, we think a lot that we will do all this in the future, but whatever has to happen, happens, we have many plans, like mine were the same, but now I have done the opposite. I never thought that I would write this book, but what God knows is not known to us and we should learn from the past that whatever mistake we have made in the past or have learned something somewhere then in the present. We should correct it and not repeat the same thing again. When god hurts someone or causes some trouble, then many people understand that God is giving us this opportunity again and again to ends our pride and ego, but when humans ignoring these things, he again falls into this arrogance and pride, then God does this to him, what should he do then, so if you all are proud and arrogant, then also keep in mind that your life is also in someone's hands. He can do anything, no matter what you do on this earth, but God is the most powerful power, you know all this, you all yourself must have meditated like a person was poor in the past and then he is poor in the present. The whole world is rich and we don't know what will happen in the future, but humans neither see his past nor his future, they only see his present that he is rich, then what will happen later, sometimes we are what our eyes show us. We believe everything to be true, like now this place is very beautiful, then that place is completely dirty, that is, this is the reality which is present, we always believe in this, what do you all believe and like a person is loving an animal which I saw that the person is kind and lovable. Then the same person is killing the animal, another person saw it, due to which that person became dirty and bad, hence mostly we consider what our eyes show us as true and only after seeing the eyes, we remember that person in our mind. Thoughts come to us that how is he present and eyes play all this role. Now maybe we have a house, a vehicle and no one else has it, then we will feel that he has it, he has nothing but times are like this. Which is easily found, the house of the previous person and the vehicles have become old, which only the earlier humans have seen, now the other person has many times what we are seeing, it all depends on the present, whatever we have. Therefore, no person should be disappointed, what is new today is old tomorrow and everyone has to get it in time, just like our body, understand that it also keeps changing, time is like this, we should be happy with what we have got. Because this keeps our mental mind calm and we do not get greedy, now we are beautiful, everyone has seen it, even if tomorrow becomes ugly, everyone will see it, that is why a person leaves all this aside and just looks at what is there now. Whatever you think next or you all know, this is just my thinking.

I know all of you are roaming in the maze of time. When I think about where the time goes with every nanosecond, where has all the time that we have spent till now gone? When my mother and grandmother tell me about their childhood, it seems that everything is back to the same place. Only with the progress of time, development is taking place in that place and their body is also changing with time, but their mind has all the memories from childhood till now. It is also very amazing when we are alone and get lost in those good memories, then we feel very relaxed and a smile appears on our face. We get lost in that very moment, no matter what kind of moment that memory is, but when we come to our senses and look around us, only we are left and the happiness on our faces turns into sadness. To know more about this time, I remain in this dilemma.

18. All the problems of women

All you women know. After birth, when we start growing up, we all have to face everything. Both men and women perform responsibilities, but apart from all these responsibilities, there are many things which all of us women have to face, it can be anything of ours, now in this I have already told about the period which is we all are so troubled in this too, but apart from this, there is a lot more which I want to tell in the second book only. First let me see how much love this book gets from all of you, only then I will publish the second book and write it these days at bed time. But many thoughts come to my mind when I realize how much pain we all women have to bear. We bear the pain even during pregnancy and then when the child is born, many women who are unable to bear it die due to liver pain. Whether the child will be through operation or normal, but even then it would be so painful, I will not say much in this book right now, I am thinking that there is a lot to say about pregnancy, there are more things to say which you all have to read but maybe I still need to know more, after knowing which I will write in the second book and then I will see how many people will support my thoughts written in the second book, so consider this book incomplete because there is still a lot to be written in the second book. I will write only on this and then if you all like my book then maybe I will write more books.

19. The reality of the book

Thoughts were coming to my mind for a long time. Then one day suddenly it was afternoon, I felt like writing all that and I went to the shop and bought a notebook, then I just kept writing whatever thoughts I had, then I thoughts that since I have written so much, then this after all the books are published, they can go all over the world so that whoever comes can read and understand the thoughts of my mind and I am happy that you all have been able to support me so much. I am writing all these things now because instead of saying it later, you everyone will understand now, I just pray to God and when I told someone about this book, then he said that you are doing it to become famous, you will become famous among all, then I told him that if anyone writes something and gets it published. If he is doing this then he expresses his views in front of all the people. Now if people like his published book, then they give all their love and if they don't like it, it depends on them. Similarly, I have written this book which is famous. Not for the sake of being famous, but whatever thoughts and ideas have come to my mind should reach you and you can understand my point. This is my aim only because how famous it is when there is pain in the body then everything seems useless and then there is death. This is only asked when one cannot bear the pain because it is not necessary to be famous. It is necessary for all of us to do all these things after understanding and feeling all the things that have been written, hence my point of view is this. It means that when someone gets a book published, then that person expresses the things or thoughts that come to his mind to the people. Now, how people liked his book, it depends on them all and how you all like this book. Because every person has his own behavior and his own thoughts, but I will be very happy that everyone has this book and is able to read it. May you all and your love always be with me and mine for all of you.

20. Sexual freedom

Transgender is also happening in today's world. In today's era, there are many things related to gender. Everyone believes that in this world, only men and women have a bond, but in today's era, there are also homosexuals who, due to the fear of the world, do not stop their relationship. Although many people accept this relationship without any fear, many are not able to do so because there are many compulsions which you all know but it is God who has created them. This is not wrong, according to me, it is right, if they are like this then what if they are also human, what is important is that a man will only love a woman and what happened to a woman and a man who are homosexual and their hormones. They are also naturally like us and you are everyone's, so look at all of them as human beings, do not discriminate because if we accept this relationship in a few moments of life, then what will happen, rather the respect in their mind towards all of you will increase. And because of this, the few moments that will be there in their life, they will be able to live their life openly without any fear or hesitation because tomorrow may not be there, life is only for a few moments, so please all of you accept them and rather only that. No, whatever the gender, you should look at them only from the human perspective because God has created every human being. Every person has his own passion, desire, hobby for any work, which is everything for him. Now is it necessary that that work should be done on the basis of gender, then absolutely not because for a person, that work is important. Gender is not important for an artist but his art is, no matter what his gender is, a person is called an artist for his work, there are many people who choose him to work only on the basis of his gender. It is said that that person has no interest in that work but this world society laughs at him and teases him if he wishes to do work based on the other gender instead of working on the basis of gender. Instead of supporting those thoughts that everyone likes, you all make fun of him. Hey, just as you all have a hobby and desire for some work, so does he too and if you all do not like his work, then you all do your part in this. Change your perspective of dirty thoughts because just as you all love and respect your work, similarly those thoughts have love for their work because the feelings, emotions, pain that you all have in me is the same in those thoughts. That's why the day you all will see the work of those poor people, then on that day the issue of gender will not matter, hence consider every work equally and not on the basis of gender, it will be very good for everyone, otherwise whatever works is done on the basis of gender. If you make fun of all these then also remember that God sees everything, lest something worse than this happens to you tomorrow because instead of looking at a person's gender, we should look at the human being, we should look at his work because God has made all human beings. But humans have created so many dirty ideas on the basis of gender because no matter what the gender of a human being is, the feelings, pain, tears, emotions of all of them are the same, hence treat everyone as equal and do not make them realize that they have to face so many problems just because of one gender. How many atrocities are being committed on them. It is everyone's life. I hope whoever understands this will be very happy. I have to tell you more about this topic but I will complete this topic in another book.

21. Relationship

This word is also very good, whose importance you all know. There are so many people in the world, but we always care about those who are our own and the unknown people we meet in this world also become our own, but for me, you are ours. Everyone is ours, as if all are ours for God. How wonderful this relationship is, when someone from our family is in trouble, then we also worry about them and sometimes it is not necessary that there is a blood relation, that is ours. Sometimes even unknown people do something for us that they also seem very close to. For me, the one who understands our happiness and sorrow and most importantly understands us, I also like such people very much. And in a relationship in which you do not get respect, it is right to leave that relationship because you respect them in the relationship and they insult you. No matter what the relationship is, someone in it repeatedly insults you and puts you down again and again. Try and you don't say anything to him so that this relationship continues, then are you happy in such a relationship? Is this relationship worth it? End such a relationship because there are many people in the world who will meet you but your lost time will not get back. Therefore, he will feel that you never want to leave him, no matter what he says to you or does to you, but there is nothing wrong with him because you are bearing everything, not him, so move ahead and we will meet and be happy because of someone don't let yourself be humiliated.

Sometimes a relationship can be anything, but every time the people of the world ask what is this relationship about, we have to give a name to a relationship, only then the people of the world accept a relationship as "Relation of the mind". Also, this relationship is very lovely because everything depends on our mind, whatever it may be, it gives a lot of relief to see whatever thing the mind gets attached to, no matter what the relationship may be, but by forcing someone into it, the relationship cannot be broken. To create and live life in a relationship with an agreement in which no one is happy. What kind of relationship is that? No matter how far away the person is from us, our concern for him should always be our love because we cannot force someone to enter into a relationship. Instead, you should see such a relationship which will respect you with true heart and not out of any compulsion or greed because those who love you with true heart and care about you, then they support you in all your sorrows and joys and always support you. They are together and are maintaining a relationship with you out of greed. When you do not fulfill his demands, he will definitely leave you and a relationship of compulsion is like forcing someone and taking advantage of his helplessness and establishing a relationship with him. So what about such a relationship? The advantage is that he may be with you in a relationship but he will never be with you from his heart because you have forced him into the relationship, hence only that relationship is the one in which there is no compromise, greed, compulsion and in which everyone is happy. A person starts loving another person only because he gets everything he needs, but he does not have any bad feelings in his mind because how can a person become such an important person for another person? That person becomes so special for him, he must have passed through those paths many times where his house, shop or anything else is but when he gets everything that he wants from that special person, he keeps getting attracted towards that person but he loves her and loves her and his family too. Like when we meet a person, he is understanding our words and understanding us and then it is not necessary that this relationship reaches the body because it is of the mind which we love if we consider the person good. The relationship should not end with the body only, because if you love the relationship you love then the mind will become very happy even after seeing it. There are only a few people in this world who do not misunderstand the relationship of the mind, but there are many people who call this relationship wrong and start making unnecessary statements. In the life of all of us. There definitely comes a person with whom we have a bond of mind. When the bond of mind is established, then we love and care for that person so that he/she is well and every moment we only pay attention to him/her and by thinking about him/her we remain happy all the time. We have no desire to get him because we have only a of the mind relationship with him. I get a lot of relief just by looking at him and by spending time with him and what you all must be feeling about who that person is, you never know when he becomes yours. After spending some time with him, it seems as if this time stops here forever, the thing which we can never leave, no matter how many times we have been told to leave that thing, but only on the advice of a special person. But our giving up something that we like very much just because of his/her request makes that person very special. Then, whether that person is older or younger in age, even if he is a married person, our love for him is always there and for the person for whom we have never worried or worried, our worries start turning into worries. It is like he comes to his shop at 5:00 p.m. and after 6:00 p.m., a very strong storm and rain starts coming and he has to go home by 8:00 p.m., then he starts worrying that he will get wet in the rain. There is a very strong storm going on, we don't know whether we have brought raincoats or not and we all start praying to God to take care of them. The relationship of the mind is very sweet because in this we all do not have any desire to get them nor this. It is a relationship of the body, it is only a relationship of the mind in which the mind of that person and ours is clear for each other and thinking about that person brings a smile on the face if you are alone and sad or are in trouble with someone. When you are troubled by something, then remember that person and remember those lovely moments of laughter that you had with him and get lost in them. Then there will be a smile on your face and you will not even know about sadness or trouble when we look at that person. When we remember the actions and words of a person, we get a lot of peace. God has also made this relationship of mind very sweet. It is said that anyone can establish rights in the body by force or compulsion but the mind can never do so. Nor in the soul we don't know at all when we will develop a relationship in our mind with which person. Consider it like a story. It's like someone has a shop. How many times have we gone to that shop, but we don't even know how many times we have come through that shop. But the reason why our mind gets attached to someone is because whatever our mind needs, we find it in that person and we can adopt him better with someone with whom we never even talked to him. By accepting and trusting him, everyone starts telling him their things or whatever and a bond of relationship is formed towards him and then whenever we go through his shop, I feel like meeting him. Let's go because seeing them and talking to them gives a lot of peace to the mind. Even if that person is at a distance of 5 minutes or 15 minutes or how close or far away but if he is not visible then he seems far away from us. Better than this is the moon and the sun which are millions and billions of kilometers away. Despite being at a distance, at least we can see them with our eyes everyday and no matter how close that person is or even if we are only 5-15 minutes away, if we are not visible than how far away he will be from us. Give a feeling and if it is true love from the heart then only that person should be happy and well then that is also fine and that person does not need anything from that person because for him only that person is precious and the relationship of the mind. It is only for the one who once settled in the mind, no one can ever take his place because there is only one mind and only he is there in that mind, hence this mind relationship is not wrong at all. One person is married and has children but the other person does not care about all this because he considers the married person to be good. If you love them, then their family also becomes your own and that person has love for that married person only because his behavior is very good, it is exactly what he needs and he understands that person.

They respond by listening carefully to everything and are intelligent and the other person also cares a lot about them and that married person is a good person, then this relationship can also be a relationship of the mind which will be there for many of you, hence just this relationship. It may not only be physical, there will be a lot of such relationships among all of you, but sometimes the people of the world misunderstand this relationship because maybe they all have dirty thoughts in their mind, but it is true that some people among all of you. There will definitely be such people whose relationship will definitely be a relationship of the mind and there is nothing wrong in the relationship of the mind, a relationship which is not tied to anyone that this is mine or someone else's but still we all know it. But perhaps that married person has only this in his mind that what will someone think but there is no wrong thought in the mind of the other person, even if it is his child, then he is also the child of another person and his family is also different. A person has a family and just as he loves his family, similarly for another person,his family has become his own because everything that was thought in every human being till now was found in him only, but in this world this mind the people of the world also consider the relationship as wrong due to which one day one has to accept everything. Reluctantly and move ahead, but if you think about it, this time is passing every nanosecond. This is a planet, this is the Earth, but due to dirty thoughts of people, one is forced to end that relationship too. My mind does not want to get separated from her at all, but maybe that married person is also scared because he too is in the midst of dirty thoughts of people, even though he is also happy. But because of the dirty thinking of the world, he thinks that the people of the world should not defame him, should not spoil his image, position, then the other person thinks that even if that person understands me, but then that person feels that it is a forced relationship. The one whom he then destroys, my heart cries a lot thinking that we got separated even though we did not want to. Sometimes in the relationship of mind it seems that why did it happen only because of this, it could have happened to someone else also but this is the mind, now it has come so what to do when we are alone and lost in their thoughts than we don't even tell. It can feel so good but when we think that the time is so sweet now and one day this time will pass like this and then only memories will remain, all the time spent will be remembered again but they will not be in front of us, we will miss them and talk to them. We will feel like doing something, we will feel like seeing them, but one day due to the dirty thinking of this world, we have to separate and then we have to leave their path, which we had started following, even unwillingly. In the relationship of our mind, we start believing that we have complete rights on them, but when we think about whether it is right to have so many rights on them or not, is it wrong on them because we do not know what is in their mind, but if someone is married. He is a human being and his child is also there and we are feeling that if it is not wrong then we can tell him but we should not force anyone, we told him and he does not have any objection or problem then it is right. You talk to them without any worries and leave the fear of what the world will say because you are also right and that too because this relationship is only of the mind, nothing of the body, so there is nothing wrong in it, all of you, be open because it is a relationship of the mind. We all get to meet very few people and never lose what we have got because whatever you want is in that person because life is only for a few moments. How long do we have to live like this in fear that the world will think this? Let the world think because when you are alone or you need someone, then the people of the world are not there, then only the relationship of the mind is with you and this relationship is always with you everywhere, even in the memories of all of us, but sometimes forcefully. Or never force a relationship, it is a "Relationship of the mind".

Today I would like to tell you about a person who never scolded me, let alone beat me in life, he just explained with love that since we were little, we used to go to my parent's house only. And then we started going to school. Even when it was Sunday or any other holiday, we always used to go to my mother's father's house. I liked it very much there, the river is at a distance of 200-400 meters from there, it is the holy place of god. The view of the river from there is very beautiful. When we were young, there was a small farm and garden at our grandfather's house in which guava, lemon and other flowers were grown. Then brother and I used to climb the guava tree and pluck guavas. At that time, my mother's father used to scold both of us so that we both do not fall down from the tree and do not get stomach ache by eating raw guava because he is the one who gets and scolds us too, who cares a lot about us. I wish that time could come back again, even now whenever I go to my mother's father's house, I still like it very much there and I was 9 years old when my mother's father died, I miss him very much. I remembered because he loved me the most and whenever there was any festival, he used to bring a lot of things for us and that person is my beloved mother's mother who never beat me and never even scolded me, till now she always loved me. And they care about me a lot and explain to me.

I was getting vaccinated at the time of corona. After getting my first vaccine, I came home and lay down. It was afternoon and then by evening I started feeling very cold and I covered myself with a lot of blankets, quilts and covered my whole body, head and hands, legs. I was having pain, my brother and mother were applying balm on my hands, feet and head. At that time I was unable to bear the pain and then I held the hands of my brother and mother and endured the pain. It felt like today. So death is coming, then it happened at night, till then I was lying in the bed, I had just eaten fruits and snacks, then after work, my father also came home, at night I felt pain again, then mother and brother helped me. They took care of me and fed me water with a spoon while I was lying down, but if you think about it, what was so special about it, it was that on the day I got vaccinated, my mother also got vaccinated on the same day and brother a day before but both of them expressed their pain. Without seeing, he saw my pain and dad also took care of me, due to which this is also a relationship, with whom we love, then this is love for me, then the one who understands the pain of others without seeing his own pain, then this is called true love and love. For anything, it can be family, relatives, friends or things like this which I love very much.

"True relationship"which is not just a blood relation but a true relationship is one in which a person's emotions and feelings are always there for that person because no one is able to understand what you all feel and what you all feel. Emotions are there. When a person feels pain, that pain is felt by all of us too. I will tell this relationship through a story. There are two people, both are strangers, they do not even know each other, but whenever they meet, there is hesitation at first, a little uncomfortable. But with time, understanding each other, a feeling of being one's own, worrying and taking care of each other and loving each other a lot and I will not tell the age of anyone in this because there is no age of relationship, this emotion that a person sees has no age. So still I would like to explain this relationship, understand and feel this relationship because it is the most deeply important relationship in the world which can be understood only through emotions and feelings. When we know that despite having so many people in this world, there is no one word we can call our own, everyone who was ours before has left us and gone from this world forever and will never come back. There are only tears left in the eyes wondering who we will call ours now because everyone in the world is selfish who has to fulfill their needs and this world will not be called ours without any meaning, only then someone comes in the form of hope, then after seeing that person, this feeling is felt. May it seem like one's own, may there be a feeling that without fear, then one begins to feel that this is one's own, who loves us without any meaning and without greed, takes care of us, takes care of each other, then when will the threads of this relationship break with each other? We get so tied together that we don't even realize that no matter what happens to each other, it makes a difference to both of us. This feeling, these feelings, tell everything when a day comes when we are forced to separate again, even if we don't want to. When one has to leave the other person, that feeling of separation is so intense, it breaks us all. It seems as if life has gone out of the body today, the tears do not stop from the eyes and that pain is felt by both of them. Because where have gone those moments that we spent so many happy days together, that every moment that both of us spent together, at that time there is a lot of pain, the injury is such that even we cannot heal it and the pain is such that we cannot even show it. Because I don't know where the injury happened but this body has become lifeless. Due to this pain of separation, many stay together after every effort and stay together in this life but these memories always remain but many people are like this. Those who get separated even after meeting in this relationship and because of this they are never able to forget the memories, they remain like a wound in their life. After getting injured, the marks of the injury fade away, but we can never forget that incident. Similarly, time keeps moving forward and the age of this body also increases, but those memories always remain the same and may be searched for again. That hope should be found and living on this hope should become the only purpose because man comes into this world alone but man is bound by relationships and society which are the rules but by forgetting these rules, he forgets the bonds of society or it can be said that it is just a relationship and nothing else, whether it is of feelings or emotions, but when a person's love for whom become so deep, we all ourselves do no know at all. In this world, a person loves himself the most, but if if he loves someone more than himself, then it is a true relationship, not just for show, but if something happens to that person, then he should say to god that before anything happens to him, something should happen to him because he loves them so much. That he cannot even think that something happens to the other person because he is always happy to see the person, even if he is far away, but at least he has this feeling and if something happens to him, he will not be able to bear it because these eyes are she always becomes happy just by seeing that person and her whole body becomes relaxed. When that person is not visible to these eyes, will not be felt anywhere, then who knows what will happen, that is why true relationship is the deepest relationship because in it you have the most love for yourself. More than that, we only think about them that whether they are near us or how far away they are, they should always be fine and if God does something to them then do it to us first because we will see them whom we all consider good. The world is such a big world, we are so many human beings, but we all have the same feelings, but in this life there are so many compulsions and we have to face so many situations. Because in this life we may meet once or many times but we are not destined to be together forever, God knows how many blessings come our way and everyone has their own compulsion due to which no matter how long we are together, we have to move forward one day. It happens because there is only one life but there are many ways to move ahead in this one life, after understanding everything, we all have to choose one path and move ahead and if we look back, that path gets lost somewhere in the other paths, but that the path is always remembered because that's why it started from there, no matter where it ends, that's why true relationship is such a relationship that we all can never forget in our life, this feeling, we don't know when this emotion will become whose. All the moments we spent with them in life are remembered by all of us, no matter how far away we go from them, but the time given by them is always with all of us, whenever we are sad or feel lonely. Remembering the time spent with him, it feels as if he is with us, it is a joy, which perhaps while reading this, you all must be remembering that person too. If you are, then he is the same person with whom you have true love. There is a relationship because whether he is far away from you or close to you or away from you due to some compulsion, but the person whom you are remembering and feeling is the true relationship of all of you, just as the behavior of all human beings is not the same, similarly we all have the same. Compulsion and circumstances are not the same, similarly in this life we never know where fate will turn, but that person is always remembered no matter where life takes a turn.

22. My Mind

When I see many incidents on this earth, then I feel that there is nothing, we humans have cruelty, atrocities, ego, greed and many more, then my mind becomes very disappointed and I don't care about anyone. There is a fear of taking something by fraud because it always comes out somewhere. We cheat someone and take something from him, but God sees everything, that is why he does bad things, but some people steal even under compulsion. Only when there is a need, everything in this world is bought with money. Someone is wearing very nice clothes. He is rich. He has everything. Someone is wearing old, torn clothes. He is not rich. Seeing the many rules of the world and many accidents. And after seeing and hearing this heart - wrenching story, my mind becomes very disappointed and sad, then I think that I wish there was a world where there would be a world full of nature, all the people in that world would always be happy. There will be no sadness, flowing water, lovely birds, animals, trees and plants, lovely weather and everyone's happy mood. I feel very happy just thinking about it. If it really happens then I will definitely go. Who among you all would like to go? And God, nature, universe is close to me because he will never leave me. Whenever I feel sad then I look at nature which gives me great relief and about my life I don't know what will happen in the future. Whether you like it or not, but god knows who has created me and when I think of the universe, I think that this earth is a planet in which we and all other living beings live, then when I imagine the universe, I think that there would be a world where but these are just nature and cute animals, birds and I am not just any human being, sometimes after thinking about the behavior of all these human beings and seeing and hearing other cruel and heart - wrenching incidents, I feel that now I know something about myself too. I want to tell you that perhaps there may be something of my childishness involved in this, I also like fairies very much. Since my childhood, whenever fairy tales or mermaid stories came or in movie cartoons, I used to always watch them, but sometimes even now I watch them. I think that I wish there was a fairy world in which I too would live with all of them, but in that movie or story, villains were visible to some or the other, but in my fairy world, there would be no villains, everyone would be the same, with joy, love and in that. I liked the one who used to show the whole room inside the flowers. I like nature very much, hence I have also planted trees and plants all around in the balcony of my house, on the terrace, and spend time with them by talking to them everyday. It's so relaxing to spend. And when I lie down on the terrace. And up there in the open sky, I see birds, butterflies and other things, then I feel even more relaxed, then I close my eyes and listen to the sound of birds, which is a very wonderful peace and I have never seen anything like this before. When flowers and plants are planted in the balcony or around the house, then all these things come in them, birds and insects, then after seeing them, I get lost in them. I like birds and rabbit white baby very much, I feel like keeping them with me, but I can't even keep it, when I was little, I used to get many birds' eggs or babies because when there was a storm, the birds' nests would fall down from the trees, then I would bring them home and then when they would start flying. I used to let them go when they used to go, but when I grew up, I felt like raising baby birds. I kept saying to God that I wish I could get it and after a few days, I was inside the house and my father came out for work. Dad saw a baby bird near the flowering plants and trees. Dad saw it and told me that I thought it was a joke. Then I went out and saw it, I became very happy and brought it home with me. Then I show that it was a baby nightingale. His parents gave it to him. When they were calling, the child was also calling. I took him in my hand and looked at him, then I took him to the terrace and left him there and started watching him secretly. There were other birds coming near him and then his parents. Also came to him and he was able to fly only a little, he was very small, then my father started saying leave him, I refused that I will keep him with me but he started scolding and said who will take care of him because if we all go somewhere who will take care of him when he leaves? But I didn't agree and wanted to keep it too, so I gave it to my neighbor's girl and said that when my father comes from work at night, you keep me. During the day, but at night, as soon as her father comes to his house, while getting down from the bed, his foot falls on the child and he dies. They all told me, I couldn't believe it, I thought they were joking but it was the truth. I felt sad. I told my mother that the child had died. She went and the next day her parents were calling, then I felt that the poor people were searching for their child which was not there and some children who were playing saw a baby bird and they all started catching it, then they all caught it again. I made him sit, meanwhile he started running away and got stuck at a place, I took him out from there, then I picked him up with my hands, then looked at him and he was the child of the nightingale, even then the nightingale was making noises, seeing which I understood that the nightingale was this one. When I was shouting, seeing that child just like that dead child, I felt that even though we get disappointed by someone's departure in life, God has created many similar things which we can be happy to get again and sadness, happiness, this is the cycle of life, then I was very happy after finding that child, held it on my chest and loved it, then my father came from work, looking at that child, he said that he has not left it yet, then I told him about yesterday that he the child was given to them in the neighborhood and thus he died and this child is someone else but still they were asking me to leave him, I did not feel like it at all but was forced because who would take care of him later if we all while going somewhere, someone asked me to keep that child and after a few days, the neighborhood children told me that he had flown away and one day I was outside when I saw that child, seeing whom I had a smile on my face, I am writing now. Then while writing, every moment is flashing in my mind, then still there is a smile on my face, then it went away, then after a few months, a small parrot came flying and I used to give it to all the birds outside me to eat. He ate all along with all of them, that little parrot also used to eat, which because of its colorful appearance, seemed very cute with all those birds and when it was night time, it used to come near me and sometime sleep - sometimes he would sleep even during the day and when we were doing some work outside during the day and we had something to eat, he would come to us, I used to feel very happy seeing him, and sometimes he would sleep in the trees. Among the flowers. And after flying anywhere, he used to come back to our house. My father used to scold him when he used to make noise or have fun inside the house, then I used to tell him to shut up, don't have fun, otherwise father will leave you. Then he used to understand. Then he used to become quiet and calm, some time passed like this, I did not like to keep him in captivity, I did not keep him in a cage. Yes, when he initially came, I kept him in the neighbor's cage because he used to bite, then for a day or two. After living together, I did not feel like keeping him in a cage. I thought that if he had to go, he would go away, but he did not go anywhere, he would just play with those birds and then come to us. One day my neighbor's aunty came and said, hey, this is him. He is coming to all of you without any fear. Catch him and show him to me. I caught him and showed him to them, but as soon as I released him, he flew away quickly. I thought he would come back. Some people started saying that he is still here only since that day. I had never seen all the birds eating food everyday and it did not feel good at all not seeing that parrot among them. I missed him for a long time. I was not sorry for his departure but only that he should be well because of the life which he had given him. It felt right where he felt. When I was 14 years old, the neighbor's aunty had kept rabbits, then she also had children, then when he grew up a little, then after coming home from school everyday, I took those children to my house in my free time. She used to come and love him, one day I went to aunty to take him, then I came to know that the cat had eaten all of them, then I missed him a lot, my parents are also right. You can keep a bird or a pet but you also have to take care of them. Then if we go somewhere, we cannot take them with us, then who will take care of them after we leave? Otherwise they also love all this.

During the winter time, the cat was very healthy, fat and very cute. Every night, when everyone went to sleep. My brother and I used to secretly bring that cat to the house. At that time, I was 7 or 8 years old. When I was 1 year old, I used to take that cat to my room and make it sleep with me. That lovely cat was so soft, I used to sleep clinging to it and when we got up in the morning, he would also get up and I would leave him outside without my father seeing. After he left, we also used to go to school and after coming from school, we used to spend time with that cat too. Childhood is also very sweet. Now while writing, I have gone to that very moment but perhaps that moment will come back again. May it come but it won't happen. Where have all those moments passed? Everyday there is morning and evening. Everyday time passed but the time that has gone cannot be brought back. Whenever our health became bad, Father used to boil eggs for both of us. He used to give its yellow part to eat. When my brother's health became bad, he used to give it to him to eat but he did not like eating it at all, then he used to tell me in advance to sit near me and then father would give eggs to brother. And he used to give it to me to eat with his own hands and pretended in front of dad as if he was eating it all but he used to eat only a little bit and I and I used to eat the rest and dad never knew that little we did this and after coming back from school, I used to insist on watching my cartoon, he used to insist on him cartoon there used to be a fight between us about this, then mom used to scold us, then we did not agree and then we used to have fun, then mom used to explain and then more. By the time our mother would come to beat us if we got into a mischievous fight, both of us would calm down. Once there was a big fight between us, there was destruction of stuff, then mother came to beat me. As soon as we both ran away, I locked my brother inside due to which he got beaten, he started saying that I will beat you too but sometimes brother too. They used to lock me up and I too used to get beaten, but after growing up, they again said fun, my brother is out at work, I am at home with my parents, this house is the same place, but where has all those moments spent, every single moment, gone? This question comes to my mind: can all those times come again? Is every time settled in the mind? Can it ever change into reality? Does a person's body start changing just because he grows older? But we can never forget the memories we all have. It is said that things dissolve and memories are always remembered, memories are moments...

23. God

God is the most powerful. He is the only one who runs the universe, the Earth and the living world. He is God. All the countries on this earth have people related to their religions and their beliefs and for all human beings, everything is for their God. Something happens, till now I don't know how many religions and countries must have heard the names of gods and all of you have also heard the stories, tales, beliefs based on them, because this is the reality, no matter how much we try, no matter what we think. Take but only what God knows. Like there are many people, they all have God of their own beliefs, but some people are the ones who create ruckus in this matter, they do not think that if everyone's god is someone's God, someone's Allah is someone's Guru Nanak, Buddha, Jesus Christ, then what happened to all of them, their ideal is love for God, similarly you all will have love for others and all gods, but in the name of god, many people harass Many poor innocent people, force them, kill them, oh God. Does he tell all of you that you should kill that poor person because he belongs to another religion or culture? For such people, words are useless because even my words may fall short, but why don't you all think this? That the body in which you all are proud also belongs to someone else who has given it to you, that is God's, nothing is ours, when I hear or see such stories of cruelty, then I feel that maybe it is right that people god takes lives so brutally, but there are some innocent people among them. In today's world, it is difficult to understand who to trust and who not. You must have heard many stories of slavery, that because of being from a different country or religion, they. The poor people were mistreated in such a way that the soul trembles just thinking about it. And how many cruel stories have we heard inside this earth, some were raped, some were brutally, murdered, some work kidnapped and other incidents which have happened on this earth. Everyone inside is just because of money, due to greed, enmity or other things. Only creatures from other planets would be better than you humans because they might not do all this. No matter what position we humans are in, we all have to die one day and when a shroud is put over our body then it becomes a dead body and in a few moments that person goes from "is" to "was". When one day initially I had pain from stones, I was at home with my mother and I. Then I started having pain in my back, then I told my mother and then she applied balm. It was around 3:30pm. When the pain started, then the pain was not stopping even after using so much balm and massage. Then at 5:00 p.m. when my father came from work, the pain was becoming so painful that I could not bear it. I started rolling here and there in the bed and immediately took me to the doctor but the doctor did not come till 6:00 p.m. and then I called him and by the time he came, the pain was so much that I was asking God for my death. Since then I started feeling that when there is pain in one's own body, then one does not need anything from this world. That day, I myself was asking God for my death, the pain was so much, then he came, but that day something happened. I have learned a lesson, that's why I think that whatever god gives me in life, I will always give it to the needy people because I have God, nature and all of you who love me and God has created many people on this earth. Those people who cannot speak or hear, they also have sign language, just as you all have a language and you all do not know many languages, similarly God has given this language to those poor people too and many people do not have children, then they are not able to understand the language of God. They tell us to give us children, but perhaps to get the love of all of you, God has also created those orphans who are in great need of love. Now think for yourself, why does God do this? He Makes some orphans and others. If you do not give children to your parents, then accept those children, they all need your love and I have also heard some incidents of such people like in many places, when someone's parents die, they live with their relatives. Those people show their brutality in such a way that it becomes clear that in reality God has created such heartless people for whom I cannot say no even if I use words, but some families or relatives are also very good who those who do not have parents, they consider them as their own and love them very much and that is why all of you should respect your parents and your children because not everyone gets this privilege. Love them as long as you have. You all know what a parent is. Many parents become so busy in their lives that they ignore the happiness of their children. Children feel like spending time and loving their parents and consider them as their friends. But perhaps due to being so busy in their life, the child starts thinking that despite having everything, it is nothing. Then spend some time with your children too, this life is always busy, we say there is no time, but there is time. It comes out only by taking it out, doesn't it? And the time of death, that too, will come one day. My mother and mother's mother were asking us to go somewhere. At that time we were at my mother's father's house. I was listening to them. I must have been 6 - 7 years old at that time because even at my age I felt very well. I don't know why they went away. After they left I thought I would also go to them and I started going but I went towards the other way, I thought they all must have gone in the same direction, in the beginning there were houses far ahead. After reaching the way, there was an empty field, forest and river too. Then I saw some men who were building houses and there was no one there. I started getting scared as to how to go home now because of all those men. They were laughing at me. I remembered God, God help me. Within a short while, a boy was going on a bicycle from that place. He went some distance from me. Then I thought that I should react as if I would react to this boy. I know, then I called him from behind and ran very fast so that the people working there thought that he must be my own, then I came back home, after sometime my mother and others had also come, I told them the whole thing. She started saying that we had not gone that way, we had gone on another way and she started scolding me that I would never go like this again, but this thought had come to my mind at that time when I had told god that we should come somewhere alone. Can't do this, do we have to live with fear? Why does this fear exist? Just like my family and relatives are also human beings from whom there is no fear, then those who are going to do the work are also human beings like us, then why be afraid of those people and just like I am someone's daughter, similarly you will be there for all of them too. When everyone loves their children very much, similarly, other person's children to are loved by all those whom you kidnap and kill brutally or do something wrong, but for that God everyone is equal, therefore, as you and if you think and do for others, then God also does the same with people like you, because the game of time is different, today you are strong, tomorrow you are weak, that is why we say that God is with us every moment, if we believe in him with true heart, then and when. When we are in any trouble or sorrow then he is definitely with us to help us in some way or the other like where did that boy come from on the bicycle and then where did he go but little did I know that this is the beginning of my knowledge. Now god knows what situations I had to face, now as I grew up, I started analyzing everything. First I used to think that children are parents or should always go somewhere with elders, they will grow up. So, you can go anywhere on your own, but little did I know that after growing up, there will be even more restrictions on coming and going. I will talk about it in another 26 topics only. Sometimes I even think that in reality God has created such heartless humans that they kill other humans mercilessly and enslave many people. You all can understand what they do with them. There must be people with whom all this has happened. A person takes another person as a prisoner and tortures him so brutally just because he is from another country or from another religion that.... I can't say further because while writing, all those incidents and the cruelty of every human being are coming to my mind and maybe if I write those things, I will feel like crying, so you all know that pain and when a person goes to some other country. Wrong about the religion or the people there, why don't you tell this to all the children or when the child starts going to school, this is the Earth which God has created and in it we all humans live, even if everyone has a different religion and culture. If it is different then what happened, they are all humans, everyone has their own beliefs, so what is the point of fighting and killing, and when humans attack another country, not only people die there, but many people die there. Life gets ruined when bombs are dropped in a country, half of the people, perhaps after being saved, see their family members dying of hunger and thirst in front of them, and then what is that feeling, do those cruel people like you know how much trouble they face at that time? We face that laughing and playing game, that place gets destroyed with those bombs and then the nature there, the people there, everything becomes like that as you know and then all those people who had gone to the army war. One day everyone dies while fighting this war. Whether they win on this side or that side, but bye then everything is destroyed and what kind of victory is there, what kind of defeat. When a bomb is dropped, many people die there. The rest are injured and many of their families are destroyed and then one day they die of hunger and thirst and one day again they become slaves and then after becoming slaves, cruel people do so much to them. Then one day they die there too. Then has god created people like you to torture and kill other human beings like you? Then what pain would their soul feel at that time? Many of these people you too will be there and you will understand everything very well. Feeling this word "Death", everyone feels that one day I or you will have to die. Right, if a person stays away from another person no matter how far away he is or he remains angry, then the mind convinces itself that he okay, we will meet him again, but when we remember a person who has died, then the mind is very happy that he has spent his life with us and there is happiness in the mind, the mind says that once again we can share our life with him. Let me spend my life one moment again. I miss his every activity for a moment, I feel like seeing him, every moment I feel like doing an activity, my eyes yearn to see that person and the body says that with these hands I want to see that person. If I can touch him, he may come in front of me again, but this is the reality, that person who has died will never be seen again, no matter how much we cry for him, but when the shroud is put on the body, then it becomes a dead body, one day it will really happen. We all will die. A few moments ago, the same person talks with us happily, gives his love and within a few moments, that person falls asleep in such a way that he never wakes up again. How many times do we shout and cry to him - they try to wake us up by crying and say, don't leave us, why did God do this, but who can stop the one who has gone, so that no matter what position any person may hold in this earth, but for God, only that person is God. From his position “Death is the only truth and the most powerful God in this world”.

24. Stop the brain and mind

In today's generation, whether a child, an elder, an old man or a teenager, everyone gets stressed over small things, gets disappointed and becomes sad inside. In today's world, there are very few people who do not overthink all this. I am not forbidden to think. Because whatever I have written today, I have written it after thinking carefully. Before doing every work, one has two thoughts which are right, but if that work, or any other incident happens to us, then if that unnecessary thing happens. Thinking about something that may not even happen in a year or months or weeks, that it will happen to me. When I was 15-16 years old, whenever any accident happened to me, I would start thinking unnecessarily which had no meaning in the real world, but I understand you all because thinking too much also leads to some accident or the other. It is not like this, but if we waste our life just thinking about this thing unnecessarily, then not only our time is wasted, every single moment of ours is wasted, no matter where we are or where we are. Why, no matter what work activity is happening there, we are just lost in our thoughts and we are not concerned with any activity in the world. This happens because of some evil people who do their own thing. They are very happy in life but because of them some other person lives everyday life every moment. When I too went into overthinking stress and depression because of some scoundrel people, well, I will not say anything about those people because every human being is equal for me, everything is the same, but that is why blessings come out for everyone. Some incidents happen to us so that we can learn a lesson, but I believe in my God, because of those people, I unnecessarily thought so much and after that I went into stress and depression. They are also human beings; no one has ever walked before God and maybe never will. Whether a person does good or bad, he has to suffer the consequences of his deeds in this very place. I had become so depressed that every moment I felt like dying. As it seemed, because of those people, that is why I would also like to say that even if you meet an unknown person, first you should know him well, only then friendship or any relationship should be taken forward and perhaps this incident has happened with me because only then, whatever no matter how many of you are, many of them are like me, so please, there is no point in worrying. If you all keep overthinking in some moments of your life, then how will you be able to live your few moments of happiness? And in today's world no one can live without social media, internet. It is used for good works as well as for other works too. Sometimes if we get very good comments then we feel happy and if the same comments if too much goes wrong, it makes a person very depressed and sad because then he starts judging himself by those comments and he starts feeling completely alone in the world in his life of cheerfulness, but many people. There are such people who don't care what people are saying and among all of you, we hurt ourselves by those messages, comments or by someone's words, so leave such people and do it for yourself too. So live, you just so people the way they want, you do it, but once you become what you are, then see how much peace you will get from this life, but sometimes love those who truly love you. You understand your pain, everything, give time to them too, always live for others, today live for yourself also, "Happiness is the most important, beautiful life and your choice".

Once, due to some misunderstanding, I had thought things on my own, then I told the same doctor, whom I consider a good person, and then I told him all the things, then he said that you think to yourself that the other person is better than you. You might be thinking about these things which are absolutely wrong. You yourself think about these things which I thought were right. There must be many people among you who think about all those things from someone's words, messages or comments. You don't know what all you think about that person in your mind, which wastes all your time and you hurt yourself. In fact, that person doesn't even know that we have heard his words or comments. But we kept thinking all these many thoughts, if any of you told that person that we were thinking all this then he would say that I did not think anything like this, you were thinking for you unnecessarily, then we would feel that till now we were thinking so much to ourselves without any reason, but there are some people who keep thinking about other people, they do not tell them about it and they suffocate inside and die just by thinking about all those things. If you cause harm to the body, then there is no benefit in it. In this way, you remain sad inside because perhaps after seeing the injury on the outside, the person will ask how it happened, but the injury on the inside is very dangerous in which the person gets injured inside. I believe that sometimes this happens to us due to some accident, but just as the hormones of our body also keep changing with time, similarly we have to fight with ourselves not every single day but in every single moment. This is to say that God has created us and life is happiness and sorrow, it is necessary. Only then we will know about ourselves and others and especially we will get a good lesson and lesson for the future so that we never make such mistakes again and sorrows and problems also come so that God tests us, it is said with success. First of all, testing is also necessary so that when we test others, we can test them properly and God has created you all, he sees all of us and this is also right, when sorrow comes, we can identify who is ours and who is not, among the crowd of useless people.I come to know that sometimes I think to myself and talk to God and tell him that you have created me and whatever life has happened with me till now, you have helped me to learn from it and to explore this world. So now all of you think for yourself, do you still unnecessarily think about that person because of someone else's message, comments or their words that he must be thinking like this for you, he must be thinking like that, then go to hell, leave such people. There are many people in this world because of who you are not happy and you will meet people but that time will never come back when you unnecessarily think so much about someone else, that person does not care about you at all. So from this we understand that even before anything actually happens, we imagine that it will happen like this, it will happen like that, it is natural in every person of us to guess on a topic which is correct but the more guesses we make the more we guess. It is wrong if it dominates you, isn't it? The person whom we think so much about probably doesn't even know. Our life depends on every situation. "Control your mind and brain, don't let your mind control you".

25. Compulsions

I had told all this earlier that what a person becomes after struggling with every situation, which he calls compulsion. If there is any topic, then every person definitely says the word compulsion. Sometimes due to compulsion, the person does not even know how to tell anything to anyone. Inside I keep thinking to whom I should tell my helplessness, then when I feel that no one will understand my helplessness, then I only say to god, I sometimes get bored of this life because perhaps in life there are people. The need for medicine depends only on money. Even if a person is dying, medicine will not be given to that person without money because the importance of human beings is less than that money. I don't understand, sometimes I feel very helpless when I just when I think about the universe outside and other planets, then I feel that everything is good, but when I see and hear all the situations inside this earth, then I feel that as much beauty is there inside this earth, humans are also forced to give good deeds to one person for another. It is a man who forces himself. You and I too must have heard from many people that after death a man goes to hell or heaven, but my belief is that for me hell is in this earth only and heaven is for man which is his life. It all depends on the place where one lives a happy life. Many people are living in a place which is very clean and has everything. They have everything, it is heaven for them and you must have seen many people who do not even get 3 meals a day in their life. It doesn't happen that they also live their life and I don't know how many troubles they face, so it is the same hell for them.

How do people feel helpless even when they are ugly because instead of seeing their talent, many people reject them because of their body, due to which even after having talent, they get rejected and then they feel very sad. That everything comes and they refuse without knowing my skills, which you all know, but some people are very good, they do not care about the body of a person, they see his skill and encourage him.

All of you can also become such people. God has made every human being the best for every work, but if those people do not support you all, then do not say anything to those people which may force them to do something wrong because even though in the eyes of all of you he will be ugly because people like you are only concerned about his body and not about his talent and what can God do with such people?

There are people with heartless hearts in this world who take advantage of the helplessness of a helpless person and get those poor people to do many things. In today's fast life, everyone is busy, everyone is in a hurry, but maybe people like you are those poor people. Look at the disabled people who want to cross the road with only the support of a stick. When I was going by vehicle, I saw a disabled person. At first he was seen only with folded hands, then when my vehicle came far ahead. I saw that he was standing with folded hands with the support of his stick to cross the disabled road so that the vehicles would stop for some time and he could cross, but perhaps seeing the condition of that helpless person, he decided to move fast in life. People like you will ignore you, but perhaps people like you do not know that God sees everything. Today, the person who is helpless and standing with folded hands to cross the road, perhaps your condition may not be worse than this because time passes every moment. It is not the same, today you are going fast in your vehicles thinking that we should not get late and looking at that disabled man, you are ignoring it, lest worse than this happens to all of you, may time keep moving and people like you will always be there. If you people stop the vehicle for a short time, something will happen. Would that poor guy be able to cross? But even if some good person stops the vehicle, then perhaps other people coming in the vehicle will start telling them the same.

When there is going to be a war between two countries then perhaps no one wants a war but if we say that we will die for our country then many people have to fight the war even if they don't want to and what should I write for those people who perhaps it is not just words that force us to fight because without saying some things, seeing the incident happening so brutally, with tears in our eyes and a heartbroken heart, we just say again and again that we too are the same human being and the one who we live in a country and if someone from that country belongs to a different religion then they do so much trouble with him, which you all know, what do you get by doing all this, you all killed many poor people and destroyed their families. They are so cruel that children, old people and women, instead of seeing every human being as a human being, all they see is that day belong to another religion, kill them and eliminate them and they think with horror that in a place where they are so cruel lived here for years, was born here and today the people of this place are being so cruel to them because of their different religion and caste. The pages of reality open only when the reality is realized because this is the only thing that comes to heartless people like you. Hey, if you kill the country to destroy them and render them helpless, then what is the use if you drop bombs in that country because when some of them survive, then the people of the place where they live exploit them. Heartless people like you have destroyed that country and gone away, but many families are ruined in it and they say to god. What has happened, those innocent children don't even know what this fight, what all this has happened, many of them, their families, their parents die, they too are in such a serious condition, now what is the fault of those children and when they see their family separated from them in front of them and see them dying in such a serious condition. Perhaps they don't even know what this fight is for, but the cruelty of all of you has separated them all and you people go away without the bombs, but the people who survive there are left with hunger and thirst in their hearts due to this incident and then in the country where there was devastation, when they ask for something to eat and drink from from the people of their own country. Then no one gives them anything and one day they either die like this or become slaves.

Because someone's color, appearance, dress is different, religion, culture, country is different, isn't he a human being? Hey, just like you people, you feel pain, so do all of them, no matter what country they are from outside or their religion, their culture. Whatever may be their color, form but their feelings, tears and pain are all the same because God has given the same feelings to everyone because God has created human beings but all these dirty thoughts have been created in the thinking of some cruel people who are human beings. Not only does one see one's religion, country, culture but there are some good people also who consider everyone equal, I like such people very much. In this world, discrimination is created in the mind of a person, but the truth is that every person in this world a person is the same, the lifestyle of someone is different, the way of speaking is different but the feeling is the same in the heart of every person, just as we cannot change the color of blood and tears, in the same way we cannot change this truth. Whoever has created this world has made everyone equal. It is only human thinking that has separated humans from other humans. No matter what a human being looks like, you should give them the same respect as you give to others. In return, they are human beings. Will love you more than myself. There are all kinds of compulsions of a human being. Everyone has his own compulsion, no matter what kind they are, but it is only another human being who compels him, then that compulsion turns into stubbornness, resentment, anger, because that is why someone also, if one person is facing any problem with another person, then he tells him and that other person does not listen to him, remains in his pride, then the first person tells him, tells him again and again, still the other person does not listen and he forces that person, then this compulsion turns into stubbornness. We all have many types of stubbornness, which is also called pasion. One stubbornness of ours is the insistence on getting something, whether we want it or we do not want it. If there is something to be achieved or there is a strong desire to do some work or someone forbids us from doing something that we will not be able to do, then at that time we all make that goal our insistence that we will do this thing. No matter what we have to do when I was admitted in the 9th class, at that time all the students had to choose their subjects, I had also selected them but the test of the chosen subject was being conducted, so when the oral test took place, I passed it but on the day of the writing test, one day my marks were less, then I talked to the teacher that I like this subject, I want this, I don't want to take another subject, he said that writing is seen everywhere, I told him that I will improve my writing, he then gave me that subject. I gave it but everything cannot be improved so quickly. It takes time to improve everything. When all the children's copies were sent for signatures, something or the other was definitely written in my copy. Then I practiced a lot. To improve the writing, but many times it was written in my copy, but after a few months, when my copy went to be signed, that day there was nothing written in my copy, seeing which I was very happy, that day I was feeling that it is only because of my hard work and determination that I have been able to succeed today, then later on I took the same subject and my writing has improved a lot and I did not write anything in my notebook after that day and in any other class. I took the same subject everywhere, it was my insistence, which I did with dedication and hard work. We all human beings know everything, all we need is hard work and dedication in that work and to understand that work carefully, there is nothing on this earth. Don't know how many tasks there are which are difficult for some and very easy for others, that is why it is said to do the work in which you feel like it and have dedication, even if no one refuses, just that work should not be wrong due to which no one else can do it. Be forced to worry. In this life we find some people who understand us and love us and even if we have few people, there should be such people to whom we can tell about our circumstances, they can understand our sorrow and take us towards light instead of darkness. Come on, because there are many such scoundrel people who, when we are helpless, they take advantage of the opportunity to make us more helpless and take some wrong steps, but these people are very few but they are at least truthful because when trouble comes, they are truthful. People will always try to explain to you and not confuse you. This is life; it may be death in a moment, but as long as God has given you life, do something. Sorrow also comes because it is only when you are in pain that you understand the pain of another person. Every person appears happy from outside but from inside there are many people who remain scared. There is a silence because a person becomes silent in front of the circumstances because he is not able to even say some things to his loved ones openly. I can't even cry because there are some things that the family itself refuses to feel. If the thing that comes to the heart cannot be put into words to tell to the family members, then the greater helplessness is that a person is forced to do so even if he wants to. Sometimes situations arise which we have to bear and we are not able to say anything to anyone. Being is only a human being but when any compulsion comes in a human being's life then he gets very troubled by it. There is humanity which is inside every human being because kindness, love and compassion are with all of us, it is only our duty, whatever. We have got the responsibility just to fulfill it, we all do such things which we all know are wrong but we have to do it to fulfill our duty. Now let us talk about war. During this time, how much distressing and unbearable atrocities are committed on the common people, who have nothing to do with this war and all of them are made helpless from their homes and they are hunted down and killed mercilessly. And the biggest compulsion in this is that if the people who have been ordered to do all this help them instead of killing them, then they are called traitors, they are punished for betraying them and they become so helpless. They are saying that they should kill all these innocent people which is wrong for them but if they betray their country then they will be punished as traitors by their own country which shows that some heartless people who want to show their power. Who knows, they crush the lives of so many people, harass and torture innocent people just for their own selfish gains, and in this war, women have to bear the most pain because they are not only given death, but so much more is done to them. Nasty acts are committed when a person forgets his humanity and resorts to cruelty, then whether the women are of that country or of another country and religion, all these atrocities happen to the women of all countries and religions. In this war, women are when they are imprisoned then they are forced to do so and if they protest or refuse then they are beaten or even killed and they are forced to be kept apart from their children. They are separated from their beloved home and kept as prisoners in which there is no fault of those innocent human beings because we don't know from where the war started. But till the end of the war, those who never wanted so much to happen, this unnecessary war, so many dead bodies and everything, these innocent people have to suffer till the end in this war and those who talk about spreading love and peace everywhere, they have to face this it is said that strength is the best, fight war and win every situation with your strength, but as long as a person wins or loses, there is destruction everywhere and many people who have seen so much from close to themselves in this war, they never forget what they have endured, the war ends but the wounds given to them in this war never heal. On the outside, the body gets healed but on the inside, it gets completely broken, which happens again and again. He gets troubled by an accident in the war and then one day he dies. Due to this war, the life of laughter and happiness that all people used to spend with their families, they spend their lives by killing who knows how many people. How can anyone bear so much pain every moment? In their memories, the scan of war is visible that sometimes someone tortured them a lot and sometimes they were forced to do it on someone else, nothing is achieved from this war, who knows how many families get separated and how many other the house is destroyed with bombs and ammunition, which is also like our family because it contains so many memories of all of us and when due to compulsion we have to leave our house or burn it. Or if the enemy destroys everything in front of our eyes, then how much pain we feel. The most important thing is that when in a war, due to the religion of another country, everyone, whether children, old or young, is killed or taken prisoner. They are tortured by making those innocent people have to suffer so much because they belong to another country and religion, they are forced to join this war even if they don't want to, but with this power of theirs, they are able to force the innocent people to such an extent that it is not their fault but by proving them wrong. Torturing them for a mistake they have not even committed, punishing them for that mistake because the one who is wrong is torturing this innocent person and declaring the one who is not wrong wrong on the strength of your power and without listening to any innocent person. To kill him only by forcing him on the strength of this power, he also knows that he is wrong but he is proud that what will anyone do with him that he has this power but perhaps he forgets that God who is there is a presence everywhere who is doing all this today. Even more than this, what should happen to you? Because of this compulsion, we all have to endure so much and have been enduring it in this life. For some, this life is too short. It seems very big to some people and the circumstances of every human being remain in this compulsion, but if someone tortures someone then instead of watching all of you, help them all, only then this atrocities will end forever. " No atrocities on anyone. Do it and do not let anyone be oppressed because we are all the same as before God everyone is equal".

26. The reality of all human beings

In today's world, all types of people adapt to the place where they live. You all must have heard about witchcraft at some time or the other, that someone has done witchcraft in someone's house or has done something bad to them. You all must have heard such things once, well, I too had heard it, so I thought I should write about it too. I don't know whether witchcraft is true or not, but because abnormality is also present in this world, hence witchcraft is true. This is not about because the only thing is that now if you are reading this book then you should understand carefully.

Once everyone in my family was not keeping well, then we kept getting treatment from the doctor and my family does not believe in this witchcraft, then many people told us that for how long we will continue to take only doctor's medicine. You will keep eating, just ask a priest once what should he tell, then we ignored him, did not believe anyone's words, then when people started saying too much, just ask the priest once, then my mother went to him. When I asked, he told me that yes, someone has put a crush on all of you, you will have to do the ritual, but then I did not understand that much, then I started feeling unwell again, people started asking for a priest again, then a question came in my mind today. There is no such person in the world who is not sick, no matter how healthy he may be from outside, but today everyone's health, whether young or old, seems normal to me and the thing is that we are practicing rituals. Let's get it done, then after that, will we keep getting it done again and again when we go to different places, because if it doesn't matter, someone has done something at our house, no problem, we will get the ritual done, but someone will do witchcraft again and again. If he keeps doing it then will he do the ritual again and again? What kind of thing is this? I only believe in my god that yes, if someone does bad for us then it is god because there is no one more powerful than God and what that man is telling is that someone has done something. And the most laughable thing is that the person doing it is either a member of the family or a neighbor or a relative. Oh my God, when all this is not ours then why are we afraid of people from other countries? Just think, it means many times. Wherever you ask the priest, they go so far as to say that even your life is in danger, then who is yours in this world when all of them will fall into the trap of witchcraft to kill them? Then who is talking about witchcraft? In this world of witchcraft, there are many such things which we cannot say anything about and my topic is not on any witchcraft or superstition, only that when our own people use these witchcraft to kill us. If we fall into the trap of corruption then the danger will be for us and not for the rights of other countries, religions and castes. I hope you all have understood this.

When I went to class 9, I was 13 years old. I used to go to school alone on a bicycle. There was no student with me, so I had to go alone on a bicycle. When school was over, I was returning home on a bicycle. At one place we came to a deserted road, on one side there was a forest and on the other side there was an empty field and the main road was at a distance of 300 meters. I was coming on my bicycle. Two men were coming from behind on a bicycle and seeing me, they started speeding their bicycle. At that time there was no one else on the road, then after seeing him, I accelerated my cycle and he accelerated further. There was a place of God in that forest, I remembered him and then cycled with full strength until I reached the main road. I kept cycling fast and those bastards were laughing and chasing me. I also cycled very fast and when I reached the main road, I took a sigh of relief. Well, for those bastards, I prayed to God that these people be punished very badly. After coming home, I told my mother that this is why it was always my parents who dropped me and picked me up from school and from that day onwards I never rode a bicycle. Because of those scoundrels, I lost my beloved bicycle and my companionship. I always happily used to go to school everyday on my bicycle. There was another way to go to school but that was on foot, that too was a deserted way. Now if I go, where should I go? I was a child at the age of 13-14 and that accident happened. I felt that today every country ils free, there is freedom everywhere but we women are still in a prison because of these bastards who exploit women in every country and everywhere. If those bastards had caught me and they would take me somewhere and do something wrong with me and then if I came home and narrated all the incidents, what would the police do? Would they have caught those criminals or maybe those bastards would never have been able to find them but what they did to me. So, would I ever have been able to forget that incident? Probably never. It would have been a shock and if they had caught me and killed me after doing something wrong, my dead body would have remained lying at the same place. If anyone had seen my dead body, the police would have come. The case would continue like this and then one day the case would be closed like this the culprit would be found or never, but nothing could ever go wrong with me because I belong to God and god is making everything to be discovered, the reality of this world because the reality is that if someone is raped then the culprit is caught or not and the case goes on like this and one day it ends like this, but the one who was raped so brutally never goes through this. She is not able to forget the incident and the people of the world harass those who are raped and torture them because the person who is raped is someone close to her, people insult her as if it would be her fault and the people of the world do not support her. Instead of giving up, they torture her further due to which either her family members commit suicide or the one who was raped does so, but you all do not forget that God sees everyone today, all this happened to them tomorrow. If something like this happens to all of you, then because of being raped, you don't know how much you have to face, all those with whom all this has happened, you all must have understood my point very well, now due to this, the country in which you all are living. Are they executioners or people from other countries?

When I used to go to computer class, there was a wedding of the sister of a computer student. She had invited all the computer students. I and my cousin had gone to the party. The party was at night. My brother was calling me. There was loud music at the party, and due to this, I did not hear the phone ringing. Then after having fun in the student party, all of us started going back home at 11:00pm. My cousin and I were returning home in our vehicle. I was 17 years old at that time. My cousin was much older than me and when we were coming back home from the party, two more students were coming to dropus. Then on the way, an unknown person's vehicle was stuck on the other side of the road. Then we met that unknown person who helped him. Then we started coming back home. There was a forest path in the middle due to which those students came to drop us, then after dropping us on the main road, they went to their home and we came to our home in our vehicle. When I came home, my cousin had gone to her house and I came to my house. While coming home, my brother started getting angry at me asking how much time had passed and why he was not picking up my calls. I told him that because of the loud music. I did not hear the phone ring and then he started asking why he was late in coming. I told him that the party had started late and all the students had just gone home but he started getting angry at me. I was trying to make him understand. Then my mother also started scolding me, then I started feeling very bad, what mistake have I done that you people are telling me so much, listen to me, then I got angry. Then my brother slapped me for the first time, then my mother also started scolding me, then I cried and said what mistake have I done that you are getting angry at me without listening to me and I also told my mother that you are just you love brother, you are not my mother, due to which mother started crying and brother also started crying, then the real thing came, the brother who never hit me till date or always loved me, he hit me for the first time only because he was worried about me. They started crying and said that there is a forest on the way, there who can do what to you at night and you will not even know anything there and they will kill you right there (in the country whose army is deployed on every border, to save its countrymen, the people of that country do so much with every woman that I can't even say) when I realized that my brother had killed me out of concern for me so that no one would do anything wrong to me, hey! So we are not free at home, at our place, in our own country, wherever we go, we have to go everywhere with caution. That day, after seeing my brother and mother crying, I realized that in this whole world, every family needs a daughter. If you are concerned about your wife and all the women, that all of you are daughters of someone else's family. No matter who looks at the women from the perspective of their mothers and sisters and daughters, because just as you all have women at home, they too are the same women, all of you others. You do all this with women, but don't forget that you also have women at home. How will people like you feel when someone does so much to them? What I had said in topic 23, I will tell in topic 26 itself that we are still small, hence we always go everywhere with elders and when we grow up, we can go everywhere alone, but what did I know while growing up? After this, there will be restrictions everywhere when I go somewhere alone. I went to my relative's house. I went to his house for the first time. Initially, I was getting bored, but later I started liking it there. He has two children. At that time, one was 5 years old and one was one and a half years old. I was 18 years old and I started liking spending time with them. The next day they took me and their children to a park. There was a forest on the other side and some people living in the forest. I liked that place very much because I like nature very much. Now, the park which was shown to me by my relative, I and his children used to go there every evening and I also made some friends with them. Because of this, I felt even better at my relatives house and also had a lot of fun when I had fun with their children. One day we all went for a walk in the park. There, there were some teenagers who were older than the boys. They were sitting in the wall at the edge of the forest. They were sitting and whistling and doing strange things. Then we came back home but my relative told me that now it is not right to go alone like this, what happens to a young child in the park, I told them. There are other people there, he said, but he doesn't know you much, but earlier when I and his children used to go to the park, he had told me that if anyone says anything, then call us directly, but that day he was with me. When I went to the park, on the same day, those boys were also present there, seeing whom they refused me and you all know the reason for their refusal, now I am feeling very angry in saying this again and again. Because the only thing they are concerned about is whether someone might let them do something with me. Hey, we are not safe in our own country, in our own place, otherwise if those boys had not done such things, my relatives would never have refused me and not only me but all the women on this earth cannot go anywhere they feel like going alone just because of this reason. When I was in 9th class, my classmate was telling her friends that I was going home, then I came to a deserted road at a place, there some boys came and blocked my way and I was alone because some of my friends were going towards their home. She had gone and I was going towards my house, then those boys stopped me on the deserted road, then I ran fast to my house, then I said, you did not scold them, she said, I ran fast to my house. I went and said did you tell your parents? She said what should I tell you? I said I should have told her that someone will come from your house to drop you off. She said my parents both work so who will come. From this I understood that in this world no one will stay with us all the time, but we will have to go somewhere alone. When I told this to my parents, they always dropped me and picked me up from school, but there are many children in this world whose parents when children are busy with work or whose parents are not there, they are at their relatives' places, then I don't know how many of you may have faced this problem and maybe facing it till now.

Now I am talking about topic 9 when my family had told me that even if there are only two women, how many will compete with them even if they only know martial arts and one man is enough to spoil a woman's life. And even if there is only one man with the women, if he is a man then I do it now. Now read the reality of all the people of the world carefully and thoroughly, understand it like a story, I would like to tell it like a story. 2,3 are mature girls and 4, 7 are mature boys. All are friends and they all go to a forest resort for an outing. Then there are 3, 5 men in this resort, some of them are teenagers and some are mature. They all came to the resort, then they all met. Next day, all of them went for a walk in the deep forest. There, all of them had fun and at night, inside the same forest. They set up a camp but those 3, 5 man had a plan to do something wrong with those girls, then they went to catch all those girls, then their male friends came to save them but those 3, 5 man they had guns due to which they killed those other boys, now the remaining girls, after this you all know what those brutes will do with them, this gave you some understanding, I hope you all have understood from this story. What I wanted to tell you is that in today's world, many laws and rules have been made for the safety of women, but when we are not safe in our own country, then why do we call other countries dead, because if we have to make them dead, then we should do it in our own country. Make those people of the country cruel who exploit all of us in every country and every region. Rape the women of your family brutally, torture them brutally and then kill them one day. All this happens in the same country. In the country where you and we all are I agree that there are different countries in this earth, but as many of us women are there in this earth and the exploitation that happens to all of us and is happening, that pain is the same for all of us, when the pain is the same for all, then we all humans are also the same, we all have the same feelings, whatever I am today, you all are also the same, only our way of life, religion, caste, appearance, our culture, our country, are we not one because of being different, rather we are all the same. Everyone

is equal for that God, in the same way you all should consider everyone equal and instead of making fun of the people of other countries or destroying the people of other countries, first of all you all eliminate those brutes in your own country who that behind which face might be hiding a scoundrel inside him? Because there is no trust in anyone anymore, till now you all must have heard that the family members are exploiting the women of their house and many people remain silent thinking that the house will be brought into disrepute and that bastard. He does his own thing because he knows that no one can do anything to him, but thinking that the family should not be brought into disrepute, I don't know what that scoundrel will do. "Your one step can stop that bastard from doing all this, so do not think about the disgrace of the house and face every exploitation because god is with everyone".
There are many forces in every country of the world to protect the people, but the laws which have been made are to protect the humans. If he turns from a protector to a Predator, because today you all must have heard that many people take advantage of their power and exploit innocent people. Oh wow, now there is no need to destroy or destroy the people, forces and country of another country or to plan to kill the people of that country or to throw bombs in another country. No needlessly to fight because in the same country where you all are living, there are such despicable people who use their power to force an innocent person, even if that person does not commit any fault, yet they use the power of their power to force that person to fight. But you all bully, but you all remember that because of a rule you all have got this power, but for God, no power matters because God has created you all, so for God, which human being on this earth is important? It doesn't matter to him whether he has power or not, he only sees the deeds of all of you and I have already told you about the time, today he will commit atrocities on some innocent person, what will happen to you tomorrow. Many people are so stooped when they torture an innocent person that they do not even notice that they brutally kill children, women,

old people and men. What is the meaning of power when innocent people are killed? Just want to exploit it. Now the point is that it is not necessary that all of us women will have security and only then we will go out of the house because now the predators have started thriving at home itself. Because of which earlier we were not safe outside but now at home we are all being exploited, so now stop being afraid of anyone, oppose everyone openly because only by taking a step do we start walking and by speeding up our feet. We start running. Similarly, only when you oppose all these atrocities, will we all be able to be free from ourselves and all you parents as well as the schools should teach the women and children of your country about every defense so that they can protect themselves. Could. And even in today's generation many people are doing all this and support your children and teach them about every protection and if someone does wrong to someone's women then not just one but everyone should protest together because today it has happened to them. This may happen to all of you tomorrow too, that is why you all will protest today, only then the women of tomorrow's generation will be able to go anywhere alone without any fear. The fear that we all endured will never happen to them because they if you kill all the beasts, eliminate them, erase their names and traces, then there will be no beasts left, then the women of every country will be free and whether it is night or day or deserted road, they will not have any fear in their mind. And I am talking about every human being living on this earth, which you all must have understood because it does not matter what power the scoundrel is in. There are many people with power who think that what harm will anyone do to us? Because of this, many women on this earth have to endure so much due to fear and helplessness. But there are so many people on this earth, how can so much oppression happen to one person? Even though there are so many of you, how can so much happen to someone? If you all fight together, will anyone ever be subjected to so much exploitation? Then no. Everyone remains silent thinking that whatever happened to them happened to them but why do you all forget that today the poor people ask for help from everyone and you do not support the same people for justice. Wow, I am feeling bored. Because what can I write about this earth, even if I keep writing, then I don't know when all the events of this earth will end. Those planets outside this earth who analyze the universe, despite not wanting to see such brutal atrocities on everything in this earth. My mind said that to know the outside of the earth later, first reveal the reality inside this earth. It has become a fear to trust anyone inside this earth because now whether on oneself or on others because inside the human being someone who is full of deceit, Pride, greed and jealousy, someone is very cute on the outside but it is not clear what is happening inside him, how is this world, how has God created human beings, better than this, the creatures of that universe and the planets would be right.

In this world, even if someone's house has everything, every facility, but if there is rivalry and fighting in that house, then despite all this, everything seems useless. There are many houses in this world where there are many problems, fights and quarrels. Arguments happen frequently and small children get scared after seeing all this. This must have happened many times in your house too or you must have seen or heard it in the houses around you when parents fight with each other, whether the father hits the mother or the children get scared by it. Whether it is the mother's or father's fault, but due to their daily fights, children start complaining of mental stress. Seeing all this everyday, a person gets fed up. Today, there are many houses in the world and every house has this problem. Many women are being exploited and remain silent thinking that he is my husband and if I tell him anything, he will leave me and my children and silently day not only suffer the oppression but also allow their children to be exploited. So protest, how long will you tolerate all these things? Life only ends one day, for how long will you be afraid like this, don't keep quiet thinking what the people of the world will say because what is the work of the people of the world, just to say and make things, but the people of the world are not tolerating all this that you are enduring in everyday life. Are how does a husband torture his wife so much as if that poor girl is not a human being? Even if you tell her the truth, it still seems like she is lying and he starts beating that innocent wife and she doesn't tell anyone about the atrocities. The little girl whom he gave birth to, brought up and loved so much and then dedicated one day to someone, now how much he tortures that innocent child and that poor girl is not even able to tell this to her parents so that she can be saved. Parents should not be worried about it. Many of these women, including you, spend their whole lives in this manner. Until the time we are not married, our family has the rights on us, then after marriage, it is the rights of the husband. Wow, beating your wife, abusing, creating unnecessary drama, how many family members support their daughter, but many family members avoid the matter by saying that now he is your husband, perhaps this is your destiny.yes now he is your everything, so listen all of you, nothing happens in anyone's luck, if you face every exploitation, then this exploitation should never happen again in the house and luck is not made up, luck is also our own. It has to be made because all these dramas that happen have an impact on the children. No matter how much those children face all this, how much will the children still be able to do? Only you elders will have to do it. If you all protest today, then tomorrow this will not happen in any house.

When we were children, our grandparents took great care of us. They do so much for us just to bring a smile on our face and if we get angry with them then they try their best to convince us. They try their best to feed us with their own hands and sometimes if we become unwell, they also get worried and then take full care of us, but what do we do when we grow up? They scold and beat. "Old age"which is the reality of all of us, we must have seen many all people working, which they are also doing to live their life, but is it really true that old age is coming to all of us because I I can't believe why this old age comes due to which a person becomes so helpless and helpless that then he searches for support somewhere else. The house that once belonged to him and the children whom he brought up with so much love, are now in the same place. Everyone threw him out of the house for whose happiness he used to work day and night so that he never lacks anything. Today he threw him out because of his old age because he is becoming a burden. What disgusting people they are. Those who trouble their old parents like this but you all forget the love given by them which is the most precious thing in the world which has no value. You do this with your parents but god sees everything. Today you all are misbehaving with those poor people who have sacrificed so much for you all, today you all are torturing them, but even after doing all this, these poor people always pray to God for you in their hearts. That you all should be fine, but for all you disgusting people, all this would not have happened to them because you have thrown them out of the house, now they are nothing to you, whether they live or die, it doesn't matter to you all, there is someone. It is so disgusting that one wonders what punishment God should give to such despicable people who fraudulently take over the entire will of those poor parents and leave them either in an old age home or on the footpath. He himself lives a life of luxury. What can we say about such a despicable person, the parents who loved him so much and brought him up, will support him in the future when he grows old, but support is a long way away, he turned out to be a beast who is very cruel to his children. They forget the love of their parents and abandon them when they need it. By bringing them to such a situation, it would be better if they remain childless, at least they will not have to be dependent on anyone for raising such children and this is how the executioner threw out his real will from the house, which is that of his parents. I don't know how many of them till now, I don't know how many of them, after growing old, I don't know how much I have to listen to them. There would be only a few people who would listen to the words of their old parents. We respect them and take care of them, otherwise I only heard everywhere that our children torture us, so I also wrote this topic so that you all do not forget that one day you all have to grow old and the actions that you all do. What you are doing to your elderly parents, to those helpless people, if something worse happens to you tomorrow, then you may not even get time to repent. Therefore, from now on, respect your old parents who have made you worthy of themselves by bringing up scoundrels like you, fulfilled your every need and now you all are beating them and torturing them so much. What are you doing? They are afraid even to tell anything about their home to anyone, I don't know how many things I have seen and heard but when I understood their pain then I felt that this is also very important because only if you change today then tomorrow will change for all of you and I am very happy that there are people like you who love their parents and understand them, so you can become like all of them and respect those who gave birth and brought you up, this time will come for all of you too.

Small children, those innocent people who should get the love of elders, are being exploited. What kind of world is this? Those little children who do not even know whether someone is doing wrong or right to those innocent people, means God has created these despicable people also. Who lives as a good person on the outside and is a Predator on the inside. Who exploits all those innocent children, an innocent child who is as delicate and lovely as a flower and instead of loving those innocent children, they exploit them. And all this is happening with all the children in this entire Earth due to which the parents of all the children fear that someone might do something to their child. And one more thing, all of you must keep in mind that this Predator can be anyone of your own or someone else's, because this Predator has put on a mask from outside but there is a Predator inside him, so all of you, please give good touch to your children. Tell them as much as you can about bad touches and how to be careful, at what time, what to do and what not to do. Tell them about all these schools. There too, tell small children about all these wrong things so that if someone does wrong to them then they will understand whether someone is loving them or exploiting them and because of this they will be able to depend on themselves. When I had to know the condition of these innocent children, my heart was horrified. At that time I felt that all these Brutes ruin the lives of innocent children even before they have even begun. Instead of allowing innocent children to do all the activities that every child should do, these predators do so much wrong to children. And these guns and bombs are given in the hands of many children, due to which every innocent child becomes helpless. The children who had the knowledge in their hands and their future as children, are doing so much today because of some scoundrels. It hurts so much to know all this because humans are doing so much to all these innocent children, which is happening in every continent and every country on the earth. When children reach adolescence, many questions start arising in their minds, and when they are someone, they are left in a dilemma as to what to think and who should be asked and who not. Sometimes, due to some questions, they start feeling depressed due to which they ignore other activities of their life. And just remain lost in those questions, you all understand which questions I am talking about. Because this thing definitely comes to all of us teenagers at some point or the other, the study of which we all must know. When we all are about to enter adolescence, a lot of changes start taking place in our body. And after finding this new form inside all of us, many emotional questions start arising. And then when we all start growing up, who knows how many things are said about the private parts of our body and what is right and what is wrong for all of us. We all are told about these things at home and in school, but who knows how many more such questions start awakening in the minds of all of us. So that if we ask someone, they will not misunderstand us and if we ask them who should we ask, there are so many such questions, some children ask most of their friends among themselves but after questions they get answers and then the answer also becomes another question. Then the answer was found and that also became a question because when we enter adolescence, we all have to know everything, but if we ask, then whom should we ask. Because I myself, when I was a teenager, came to our school to study what changes take place in our body when we reach adolescence, and what is wrong and what is right, but there were many questions that I wanted to ask. So who should I ask because I couldn't ask my family and they would tell even their friends whatever they knew. And whatever he said became a question for me. Then someone would give an answer and then the same answer would become a question because no one would tell all these things openly, there was hesitation among everyone. Whenever he tells me only a little and with hesitation, and a few things if I ask anyone. So they would tell me that if you don't know then I should refuse. If I don't know then they would say that they are still children. Meaning instead of giving an answer, say that they are children now and when something wrong happens to the children, then tell them that something wrong has happened to them. Hey, but when the child does not know what is wrong with him and what is not, then how will he know. Unless you all tell him that this is wrong, because in many cases a lot of things happen to children and teenagers. Because they are not told what their questions are, everyone says that they are still young and don't feel ashamed asking such things. But when you tell all the things and make them study them through studies, then perhaps all the teenage children will not have any hesitation in their mind about anything. Otherwise the child thinks that he has committed the biggest crime in the world by asking these questions, and are these questions so dirty? So please, this study should be taught in all the schools of every country and all these things should be told what is wrong and what is not, and if they ask you any question then it should be explained to them just like the study. Because once upon a time, when you were a teenager, many questions might have come to your mind. And today if you know all those questions, then someone must have told you the answer to all these questions. And someone else should tell them, now all of you too, all these teenagers. Because if these questions are not answered, the child may not know that there are people in the outside world who take all the teenagers on a wrong path and ruin their lives. That's why you all would also like to see your children knowledgeable or among all those whose life is ruined by this outside world, therefore "The right decision of life, the world has a very precious importance, and this importance is God, so all tell the truth".

This happened just when my book was about to be completed. It was 9:00 in the morning, and I was in my room. My mother was calling me, asking me to come here and see what I have. When I went to him, I saw that he had a baby hummingbird. And I was very happy to see him, so I took him to my room. For a while he was able to fly a little at home. Then I took him to the terrace, then from there I took him down. I felt like leaving him and did, but he was not able to fly. And I thought that if I let it be killed by some other creature, I would keep it with me until it can fly and then I brought it back home to my room. And I also had my period, due to which my health was also not well. I was having pain in my stomach and back also, then I gave him something to eat, he did not eat, then I lay down in my bed. And he was coming near me, sometimes climbing through the window, sometimes into the table and sometimes into the cupboard, but he was just roaming in my room. I was not going to the other room. I was feeling very happy seeing him. There was no trace of period pain. I was lying down and he was sometimes on top of me and sometimes in my hand, once I fell asleep. As soon as I opened my eyes, he was right above me, seeing which I was completely shocked. Then he fell asleep after some time and woke up again, then he was given food and water and he ate it. And had also drunk water, I was telling my mother. Mom was also happy that I would take him with me everywhere until he learned how to fly. I named him Fivu. I even showed the baby to my neighbors, and Fivu went to sleep again after having food. And he was looking very cute. By the time I did this, the day had passed and mother was also with me in my room. While both of us were talking, he spread his wings, then mom and I started saying that he got up. And I also took his picture, but he remained completely calm after spreading his wings. Mom asked what happened, when I picked him up, I saw that he was dead. I was so fond of him that he came to us only for a short time. And I remembered what mom had said when she brought him to me, then mom was saying that it is in such houses that there are fake birds. Then I told my mother that it looks like it is also real. The only difference is that we can see it moving. And there is a soul in it but when it died, it was in my hands. At that moment I realized that he too was looking like a fake bird. I was crying a lot because I had come only for a few moments. We were together only from 9 to 2:30. I was also remembering what both of us and The neighbor's girl was saying. He thinks it is very good for you, and he stayed with me only because mom was doing her work. And he was with me in my room. I was crying a lot, my mom was saying. Don't cry, maybe God has sent him to us so that we can love him in his last moments. Then I felt like crying even more, within a few moments he had become mine. The person for whom I thought so much became silent in a moment, and I missed him a lot.

This happened a day before my birthday when the pain from my stones started again. We went for ultrasound which revealed that there was a 10 mm stone in the middle urinary tract on the right side. Even then I was feeling slight pain. But she was still taking the medicine. Then on the day of pain, around 2 o'clock in the afternoon, I started having mild pain. I felt that the medicines were breaking the stones, that is why I was feeling pain. But around 2:30 p.m. the pricking pain started again. And I went out of my room and started walking. Then it was 3:00 and the pain started getting worse. I called the doctor about the stones and said that I am having severe pain. I have also taken the medicines. Are the medicines breaking the stones? Then he said if the pain is getting worse then get the injection done. Then the pain increased further and

I rolled around in bed. I was not even telling my mother because she was not well. Then she would worry about me. I just told her that the pain was getting lighter. He asked me to call my father and tell him, but I refused. At around 3:30 I called my doctor, whom I consider a good person. Called him and told him that he would come by 5:00 p.m. I am in too much pain, so I have to go to another doctor. He had also gone somewhere at that time. After talking to him I felt like vomiting. I went out, then all the medicines came out in the vomit. After 15 minutes I vomited more, then mom told everything to dad and I. The pain in the room increased beyond limits and I was unable to bear it. I started rolling again and started saying to God that I am not able to bear this pain, it would be better if you let me die and I lay down on the mat and I had no idea where I was going even if I lay down. This pain is so bad that a person cannot lie down, sit or stand. Then I got ready to go to the doctor. It was 5:00pm. As soon as my father came from work, I immediately sat on the road and sat in the vehicle and he took me away. After reaching there he did not come. I went to the same doctor. Then I called the doctor and told him that I have come, then he said that I am coming. Then I remembered my first day of stones and today too the same day has come again. That day also I was in a lot of pain. And it was almost that time, and that day the pain had already reached before the time of his arrival at the clinic. Then we had called him and even then we waited for him and our eyes were only watching him on the road to see when he would come, so today we reached right on time. But he took some time to come, but the eyes on the road were only looking at him, wondering when he would come but as long as he came. Due to the pain, I was feeling like God please take my life now. This time the situation had become even worse , eyes were waiting for him and then he appeared. My mind felt a little relieved, then we went inside and got the injection and my condition had worsened due to excessive vomiting. And the pain was still there, after the injection I was reminded of lying down till the pain lasted. I also started having pain in my stomach.

I told him, then he gave me drops and he said take rest, then I started feeling feverish, my body was shivering. Then he checked that I did not feel like getting up at all, due to the pain I remained laying down for a long time. They had also placed God where I was lying. I was looking at them and telling God how life is. After getting some happiness, so much sorrow comes, death is better than this. And when I was in a lot of pain and when I was at home, I was praying to God for this. God, tomorrow is my birthday. Please give me death because this life is also useless. In this we struggle so much with life and in some happiness comes sorrow. Then that doctor came to me and told him that everyone's life is useless. Death is better than this, then he started saying that you have to do everything for which you have been made and this idea of dying is wrong, sad. There is happiness in this life. Then he told them that dying one day, no matter when it is, is true because after a few days of happiness, sorrows come again and again. Told him that this time I had prayed to God that I wanted to die on my birthday. He started explaining to me and then he walked away from me. By doing this, it was 7:30 p.m. my pain was relieved and then again I got my fever checked by him. And told them that she was talking about dying because if there would be too much pain in the body and if the pain could not be tolerated then only death would be sought. Then I came home and was thinking that at 12 o'clock in the night everyone would start wishing me Happy Birthday. Something happened when I got a call from my brother. I told him everything, I didn't feel like agreeing without telling him, but my health had become worse than he was. I didn't tell him or there was a lot of pain. I didn't tell all this, only that my health had worsened, so I went to the doctor. Just told this. Messages from others also started coming and I told everyone. "How everyone spends time, sometimes it brings happiness, sometimes much sorrow, sometimes a lot of pain, and till date all the prayers I have prayed to God have always been fulfilled, only those things which are wrong for me in future are not fulfilled". When I was in so much pain, I was thinking that maybe today is my last day. I should tell my brother that my aim is to get my book published and give it to every person because I want every person to read this book and understand the reality of the world. Then it seemed as if God will this purpose of mine be fulfilled? My eyes were looking only at God. And tears were coming in my eyes, death was visible in front of me. Even while writing this, tears are coming because at that time it seemed that I had planned to do so much for you all. Is this my last time, I was feeling pain and was just crying, thinking that till now I have suffered so much and have seen all the things and no one should suffer all this, then I felt that we think so far ahead and worry about everything, but only God knows what will happen to us at what time, but perhaps the purpose is bound to be fulfilled, after that day we have stopped even praying to God. Now I am just doing whatever he wants, now only he knows my good and bad, whatever he wants.

27. Life

We also get some things, lessons and experiences from the circumstances of life and life itself is everything. This includes every moment, change, attitude of all of us. For example, if we do not have sorrow in life, we all become happy, then we do not even feel the sorrow of others because how can we know about the sorrow which we have never known. Similarly, in this world, happiness and sorrow always happens in the life of every human being, only then we are able to understand the sorrow of others. This life is also very precious. Everyone knows that one day death has to happen, yet there is so much pride and ego inside the human being. As you all know, today the circumstances of this life have brought me from where to where. Sometimes I think, leave it. What do I have to do, think about the world, let it go as it is and I should be happy, but my body says. Gives me and brain to focus on my future. But it is the mind which keeps thinking about you all despite not wanting to, that is why I have already written whatever I know and think. Man also gets entangled in the complications of life, because sometimes man does not even understand what he should do and from where to where fate should take him. All of you give a lot of respect to the beliefs and traditions of the place where you were born. We all want to achieve a lot in life, but some things are left behind, even after achieving all this, we miss them a lot. And as long as this life lasts, we will continue to meet many people who will teach us the lessons of life. We don't know how many unknown people we meet in this world, but God brings us together with those whom we have to meet. And who knows how many unknown faces we meet, then they become our own. Which time, after becoming our own, they also become strangers. Every human being is only according to the need of the time. As long as the person needs the person, he respects him. Very few people are there when the need ends. Those who do not forget the favor or help of that person, but some people forget everything with time. We all feel very happy to get something new in life, but remembering the past moments leaves only sadness. Because the time spent will never come back, hence we should always be happy with what is in the present, what about the past, what about the future, only the happiness of what is to come and a time spent which may never come back. At every turn in this life, we meet so many unknown people, and in this world we never know who becomes our own and when who becomes a stranger. But perhaps a person has to do something to fulfill his needs, whether it is wrong or right.

This "Life" word is small to read but while living this life one has to see each and every situation. Just a few days ago, when I was going for a walk, there was a jam on the road at one place. And it was raining, we were inside our vehicle, then I looked outside the vehicle and there were people living in very small huts at one place. And there was a lot of mud ahead and the garbage we hate. Some human being was cleaning the same garbage, which we humans are all the same but God has given life to this human being different from everyone else. Our way of life and the work of all of us, as per my view, were small slums, but they will be very important for the people who live in them because the perspective of human beings is different. Just as our home is dear to all of us, no matter what it is like, similarly for those people too, it is their home, in which there is a lot of peace and comfort, even if we go to someone else's house, still somewhere. There is little or no hesitation. But we have our own home where we can do anything. Our home is also like a friend. There will be many people among you who talk to themselves when they are alone at home. Then you feel very good and sleep is also important in human life. If we do not sleep properly, many disease's start occurring in our body. Every human being likes to sleep peacefully but still there are many places where there are daily battles, bombs, gunshots and noise and who is the "Human"who does all this? Those poor innocent people whose life passes through this painful moment everyday, this is also life. It is also the human beings who face this tragedy everyday while staying at their homes. Peace and tranquility might have been there earlier also but because of some human being all this is happening at that place now. When clouds appear everywhere in the sky, everyone says that the sun has not come out today, the moon has not come out, but no one understands that the moon, the sun and the stars are hidden behind those clouds. The moon, sun and stars always come out at their own time, but are hidden behind the clouds. Same thing happens with humans, when a good person thinks of doing something then many dirty people do not allow him to do that work. And we suppress it with our power, then it also gets forced and hides. In this life, the times of all of us are so happy, we are never able to think about what the tomorrow will be like, but when this happy time passes, later come sad times. Then it seems as if where has all this time gone, the moon, the sun, the weather are the same, but something has definitely changed. What is that, then it is our body which will keep changing at its own time. In this life we have to face so many struggles. Sometimes I get very disappointed when I feel that maybe I don't have much time and when I am not able to get well even after taking medicines. Am. I am writing all these things right now when I feel that I am able to feel it. It is the month of August. When I look out of my window, I can see trees and plants moving their leaves when the wind blows. Is. And there are some clouds in the sky and the sun is setting at this time. Everything is very beautiful but I don't, when I remember my first time, it feels so much better when I was not sick. Then I could eat whatever I wanted and now I have to eat only what the doctor has told me. Due to which now I can't even go anywhere. I was thinking this some time back. Sometimes my life seems very short to me, perhaps seeing these circumstances is the reason why I have to publish this book now. I want to do a lot for you all but.... What can I say, perhaps not even words, but a lot right now. There was still writing to be done which you all had to read and understand and feel, but with the blessings of all of you, I will be able to write more, and perhaps I will be able to do whatever I want to do. Today, I started writing after a long time. By the way, I have got everything in this life. I got what was right and what was wrong. I did not get it, it is all God's will, because only he knows our fate, not us. When it seems that this is my last time, then there are tears in my eyes. They come not thinking that death is near, just thinking that whatever has been happening in the world till now will continue to happen even after my death, due to which I become very disappointed and frustrated because when I say goodbye to you all. If I do whatever I want to do, even if death comes after that, then it doesn't matter, because as I thought at that time, now I want all of you to be in the same way, rather everyone will consider all human beings equal as everyone is equal for God. Similarly, for all of you also that person is just like you. Now my health is a little better. It was raining continuously everyday and even today it is the time of sunset, but today I am fine with the weather. Light rays are visible from the sun. There are clouds all round it. When I look from the window outside, I feel quite happy. All the dragon butterflies are also visible and everything around looks lovely. The main road is at a distance of 200 - 250 meters from my house and on the other side of it there is a forest, which because of the rain these days, all the forests, trees, plants and flowers are looking quite beautiful. But rain feels good but due to excessive rainfall, it becomes quite slippery at some places due to which we all have to walk carefully. Similarly, in this life too, we have to speak thoughtfully everywhere. You all must have heard many people saying that this person's tongue slipped or there might be many people yourself who say to themselves that at that time my tongue slipped, I should have said it carefully. But in this world we all humans have all kinds of habits. There is one more very important thing in this life and that is "Happiness" which depends on our circumstances. A human being has a lot but the daily arguments at his home and stress, battles in his life are all this. The other person has a little but he has peace. He spends his life peacefully in every situation in which he remains happy every moment. Therefore, we all human beings should be happy every moment, and should also give happiness to others by keeping them away from despair. We should never harass anyone. There is always unnecessary stress in some moments of life, arguments and fights only give sorrow and every moment. Peace by being happy. Now you all choose whatever you want. When the "thread" gets entangled, we try to untangle it. Many people untangle the thread quickly, some take a long time to untangle it, and some are unable to untangle the thread at all. This is how our life is in which there are complications everywhere at every turn and it is up to all of us humans to solve it, but everything is possible to do. We just have to understand it because every task in the world is related to everything. It is done only after understanding. If you understand everything in life then it becomes easy and if you don't understand it then you remain entangled in it. There is a transparent wall in the life of all of us which is not visible to all of us but it is always there with all of us. All of us human beings are not able to openly do whatever we like to live the way we like to live because we are human beings in reality. These days, he creates himself the way other people like to see him, based on their preferences. Even if he tries to know himself, he is still surrounded by people from all sides, due to which a person has to mold himself according to them, and then one day this life is like this. Do others like it? By not going, it ends. Whatever we are, whatever we feel like doing, ends up pleasing this society and whatever we think of doing in this life, all that also ends along with our life. So, feel free to do whatever you want to do, because if you keep thinking only about the people of the world, what you are will always remain inside you, and will never be able to come out, so bring it out. Be as you are, let the world be as you are. Would you like to remain the same forever, because this life is yours, not theirs, they should run your life, but run your life yourself because every person changes with time and circumstances, so now you too change. How long will the other person say that you have changed, one day they will also get tired of speaking and then will become silent forever, but you will experience something after getting your new form and will be happy, then you will realize that the society were you happy in the artificial life of your choice or are you happy living it the way you like it now? Whatever I have experienced or felt in my life, I have written everything so that you all can know, nothing is easy, everything takes time and hard work to do. It takes some time to complete any work and it takes many days, months or years to complete any work, only then the work is completed and by knowing and understanding it, the work is completed.

God has created all of us in this earth in which many living beings are living their lives and they all face every kind of struggle in this life. This life is like a journey, exciting and very pleasant. This is the way of life, in which we do not know what will happen in every few nanoseconds. In this life, we all do not know how much we have known and felt, our circumstances are some things full of problems. So sometimes it may have been spent happily and sometimes with some lessons, this life is full of challenges at every turn in which we all have to overcome these challenges and move ahead. Then we have to face many challenges in the future and all these challenges end only once and you all know that. Some things change the lives of people. To live this life, people ruin the lives of others for their own selfishness. Whatever God has given to humans, he finds it less in his life and he makes the rights of others his own. By force or by force of his power, he makes a helpless person helpless and asserts his rights over his rights also. Because after seeing a human being with others, I feel that I should make him my own even if I have to take someone's life. The body needs all kinds of facilities so that it can live a comfortable life, but despite all the things we have, if this body is not well then everything starts to seem useless. At a time when there were not many facilities, the body was fine and now there are all kinds of facilities, then the body is not fine, so is it true that this sorrow never leaves us all. Due to which a person goes into trouble and worry, which is that in this life, when the body of all of us is not well, then what is the use of having everything else because from outside, the person will tell his family or anyone else that he is fine. But he also knows that he is not well but his sorrow does not hurt others. That is why he lies, some lies are to give hope to someone and who knows what happens due to someone's lie.

The body is one and there are many diseases in this body which means that a person's life ends with this disease. In today's world, there will be very few people who will be completely healthy otherwise everyone is suffering from some disease or the others. When the disease does not get cured even after getting treatment, then we all start getting frustrated that what kind of disease is this that has come back in the body even after taking so many medicines. Meaning, for how long will we live only with the help of these medicines. Well, there is no question of medicines, a person will take them, but when other things are forbidden. Like I am the only one who has been asked to eat normally and so much time has passed, then do we all get restricted in other things too due to some disease in our body, meaning our body? Struggles with so many things. When a child is born, his life begins and then he gradually starts growing up. At the time he realizes who is his own and who is not, then he is brought up and his first education comes from the family. Only after that, from society and school, he learns about all kinds of situations, problems, joys and sorrows in his life and how to face everything or how to find solutions to even the most difficult things. The child grows up by understanding every situation, the time spent by him and the lessons that life has given him, and then after growing up, many responsibilities come to him. Whatever he has to do to fulfill those responsibilities, whether it is wrong or right, he does that work because responsibilities surround man and man has to fulfill them also. It is not necessary that we will get many responsibilities only when we grow up, there will be many people who have to fulfill those responsibilities since childhood. They have been surrounded by these responsibilities since childhood because the circumstances and conditions of every human being are different, due to which the lives of all of us are different. Everyone's work is different, everything is different, age is not considered in this life, responsibilities have to be handled only by looking at the circumstances. Life is very beautiful and precious too, only if the body is healthy and has all the facilities, then this life seems even better to every person. But if there is always happiness in a person's life, how will he know other things? When a person is rebuked from everywhere and he starts getting disappointed with his life, he thinks that despite being so human, there is no one whom he can consider as his own, people rebuke him from everywhere. Due to which he becomes a victim of loneliness. In this life, loneliness for a human being is like a bad dream, yet the dream will come only a few times but this loneliness is always there every moment. And this feeling of loneliness is also given by one person to another person, who starts feeling that his precious life is worthless, due to which this loneliness makes the person think unnecessarily. All the time he feels that everyone does not respect him, does not understand him, only bothers him and says a lot of things even if there is a small mistake. When all this happens from every side, a person starts getting broken. I have seen many true stories and in some stories I have seen that many people commit kidnapping. Some for some personal purpose or some other purpose, but what I found common in some of those stories was that their lives were one of loneliness. Because of which they kidnap and keep them with them so that they can get their love, support and sympathy. We can understand the one who loves him so that we can understand that just one penny is not important in a person's life because the importance of a person is much more than that. Therefore, all of you also do not force any helpless person so much that he does something which is very wrong for all of you or for him alone. God has created every human being, but you all also do the work of improving their life. Can. If you cannot give someone your love by not threatening or harassing them, then you should not harras or force them or torture them. Which he could not bear because God is also present everywhere, only we cannot see him as you all must have seen. There is a spider's web and if something gets stuck on it, then that thing is visible to all of us from a distance but that spider's web is not visible but when we go closer it becomes visible so that it also exists. Similarly, God is always with us but he is not visible only so that we can feel him. Just like the wind which cannot be seen but is felt, now I don't know what is the shape of that wind but it exists, similarly God is with you even if you feel it with your eyes closed or even if you do it with your eyes open. He is always with you all. In life we meet all kinds of people, many of whom are our own and strangers, but God definitely connects us with those people with whom we want to meet, and within a few moments, even that unknown person becomes close to us. A person says something in a few moments that shows the path of life. I don't know all of you. You must have met many people in this life whose words or actions give a new turn to our life. Maybe only for a few moments in luck but these moments become so memorable and we keep saying something or the other to God. That's why he also introduces a person in our life from whom we all can learn something, so never be sad, no matter what kind of people you meet in your life, just remember God and think that god this is why I have brought this person into my life. So that from this I can learn some lessons of my life and understand my life, keep moving forward in this life by feeling everything, no matter how many troubles, sorrows and happiness come with me, but I have to face every challenge of this life.

"The journey of life is very pleasant and very exciting. With the passage of time in this life, we all explore everything. And then one day we all disappear from this life, we don't even know anything, the world keeps going on as it is".

"In life, it is not victory but struggle that counts and moving forward in life. Success is not the end, failure is not fatal. There is only one thing that counts in this world and that is "man's courage". The courage of man who struggles with each of his life's challenges".

"The sun looks so lovely while rising and then it starts setting on time but how much did that sun do before setting because while setting it looks even more lovely and again it rises and sets at its own time.
" This is our life".
If you ever remember me, then always look at the first star, I always see it and I believe that this is the thing that I am able to see, if you all are able to see the same thing, then you are with me with me. That's why when you see him, you must say hello and think that he is me.
And I am also sending this message to all of you, that just like the moon and the sun are always with you. Similarly, I am always with you. "Saymoon"when sun and moon are combined to form Saymoon.

Note

All of you who are reading this book, share your love with me by spreading my book to everyone. Share it with everyone, because my aim is to reach every person, to the whole world, because my heart is to spread my book to the whole world. So that all of them can read it and can feel and understand the words said because these are not written words but the truth of every human being which can be known by everyone and the more books reach every human being, the more I will enjoy. I will be happy and feel that you all are with me and if possible, you all spare some time to read to those who do not know how to read, and if you know sign language, then explain it to all those helpless people in their own language. This love of all of you will be priceless for me and whoever you are in the whole world are equal to me, hence my love is for all of you. I hope you liked what I said. After this I would also like to see who is the person in the whole world whose thoughts match with mine. I am waiting for that day. Till then, by the grace of God, you and I are all well and this book after the publication of this book, I will see how much love you all have for me. If my book is liked all over the world, only then I will write another book which is in my mind, I want to write, but first, how much love you all give to this book and then only. I will write only otherwise.

Also by Saymoon

The Universe And Inside Of The Earth

Milton Keynes UK
Ingram Content Group UK Ltd.
UKHW050441230324
439902UK00015B/467

9 798224 404858